The
Tessie C. Price

The
Tessie C. Price

BY JEAN HEYN

Illustrated by Claude Howell

JOHN F. BLAIR, Publisher

Winston-Salem, North Carolina

Library of Congress Cataloging in Publication Data

Heyn, Jean.
    The Tessie C. Price.

    SUMMARY: When they are evicted from their house,
a Maryland Eastern Shore family make their home on an
abandoned oyster drudger.
    [1.   Family life—Fiction.   2.   Chesapeake Bay
Region—Fiction]   I.   Howell, Claude, 1915–
II.   Title.
PZ7.H477Te   [Fic]   79-9442
ISBN 0-89587-010-x

Printed in the United States of America
by Heritage Printers, Inc.
Charlotte, North Carolina

The
Tessie C. Price

MEG EVANS and her two younger brothers often went straight to Whitelock's Boatyard after school. Their father worked there, and they spent long afternoons just messing around, fishing off the docks or looking over the boats that came in. Today, however, they had a special purpose for their visit; their father had told them that an old skipjack had come in for repairs.

"There it is!" cried Jamie, at eight the youngest of the three. He broke into a run ahead of Meg and Lloyd, who followed him down the dock to where the skipjack was tied. "Wow! Just look at her! She's a beaut!"

"Yeah, but she sure is a mess." Lloyd whistled.

Meg was inclined to agree. The skipjack rode low in the water in front of them, scarred and beaten by the winter's "drudging." Still, she was a proud, sturdy old sailing ship. She and others like her had been a means of livelihood on the Chesapeake Bay for a lot of years—setting out in all sorts of weather to drudge for oysters, coming back to port with their decks so loaded midships that almost no freeboard remained. Once skipjacks had been a common sight in the waters off the eastern shore of Maryland, but nowadays there were precious few of them left.

Jamie had dropped his books on the dock and jumped aboard, and was peering down the skipjack's open hatch.

"She's had some hard knocks all right. It'll be a job to get her back in shape!"

"Dad can, if anybody can. Cap'n Noah says he's the best boatbuilder on the Eastern Shore." Meg plopped down on the dock, letting her long legs dangle over the edge. Her mother had started letting her wear slacks to school, and she was grateful. Skirts were worse than useless around a boatyard. Besides, at fourteen Meg was tall for her age and thought she looked silly and gangly in dresses.

"*Nellie Byrd.*" Lloyd squinted to read the name stenciled on the skipjack's trailboards. He pushed his thick-lensed glasses up on his nose with typical eleven-year-old impatience. His glasses were a constant bother to him. They always seemed to be getting dirty or slipping around out of place, especially during his rambles outdoors. His hair was a bother, too. It was sandy colored like his father's, but thicker, and it hung in an uneven bang that often got in his way.

4

"Dad!" Lloyd spotted their father working on a crabber at the next dock.

Seeing his children, Tyler Evans came to join them, wiping his hands on his pants. He was a tall, lanky man with a deep tan and far-seeing, pale blue eyes. "I mighta known you'd come by today! Well, what d'you think of her?" He pointed to the skipjack.

"I like her a lot, Dad," Meg said. "Sure, she's scraped up a bit, but—"

"Where'd she come from?" Lloyd interrupted.

"She belongs to an old waterman name of Ed Barstow. He and the *Nellie Byrd*, they've gone out together drudgin' for more'n forty years. 'Take yer time with her,' he said to me. 'We'll not be settin' sail again till the geese and swans come in for the winter.' It'll take time, all right. Her hull's pretty bad."

"How can you tell?"

Their father laughed. "She's sinkin', that's how. She's already lower by a foot than when we tied her up. Most old boats have dry rot and leak some, but she 'pears t'be an aggravated case. I reckon we'll have to pump her every day just to keep her afloat."

Meg had pulled a piece of paper from her school bag and was busily sketching the skipjack's outline, her gray eyes scanning with keen appreciation the *Nellie Byrd*'s sturdily built hull, the graceful lines of her prow, and her lengthy bowsprit.

Her father was gazing out over the Bay with a dreamy look in his eyes. "When I was a boy," he mused, "the Bay was thick with their sails. Now these old skipjacks and bugeyes are gettin' scarce as oysters' teeth. If it weren't for the law against drudgin' with power certain times, I reckon they'd all be gone."

"What'll happen to this one?" Meg cocked her head to one side as she studied the ship's rigging, considering how to get it all down on paper.

"Not sure as I know. Barstow's 'bout ready to retire, can't afford to fix her up anyway. Cap'n Noah kinda took a fancy to her. Wouldn't be 'sprised if he made Barstow an offer."

Jamie, a restless boy with lively black eyes and dark curly hair, had seen all he needed to see of the skipjack. "Lloyd, let's go net us some minnies so we can go fishin' tomorrow after school."

"If you've a mind t'do that," their father said, "you'd better get started. I'll just finish settin' the glass in the cabin of that crabber. Then I'd like to head for home. It's been a long day, and your mom won't like it if we're late for supper."

Meg stayed behind by the *Nellie Byrd*. She couldn't get the angle of the bowsprit right, and the boards of the dock were getting harder and harder against her bottom. She laid the paper aside and stretched, leaning back to catch the sun on her face. The *Nellie Byrd*'s fifty-foot mast swayed gently in front of her, outlined sharply against the bright April sky.

Some minutes later she called out, "Look at me!"

Mr. Evans glanced out of the cabin of the crabber. Meg was clinging to the top of the *Nellie Byrd*'s mast, her arms and legs wound tightly around it. The red ribbon had come off her ponytail, and her long hair streamed out behind her, a dark banner in the wind. She let go of the mast with one arm to wave to him.

"Lord almighty, Meg!" he called, scrambling onto the dock from the crabber. "Come down from there straight

away . . . and take care! You're apt to break your fool neck!"

Lloyd and Jamie, hearing the shouts, came running.

"Wow, Meg!" Lloyd said. "You've got a nerve!"

"You can see forever from here. I can see right over Barren Island out onto the Bay."

"I don't care if you can see the western shore!" her father said. "That's no place for you t'be."

"I'm okay, Dad. I'm holding on good and tight." Meg was thoroughly enjoying herself.

"Meggie, come down," her father demanded. "Come down so's I can get back to my work. I'd not feel easy leavin' you perched up there like a confounded sea gull!"

"Oh, all right." Hanging onto the port stay with one hand, she wound her legs around it, then let go of the mast and slid down hand over hand. She jumped from the boat's deck to the dock with the ease of a cat. Her father sighed with relief.

The following day the boys again headed for the boat-yard, their minds on fishing. Meg took the bus home. She had big news to share with her mother: her sea gull sketch had won a prize in the high school art show.

The bus rattled over the loose planks on the one-way bridge connecting the two parts of Hooper's Island and stopped on the blacktop road just beyond the bridge. Meg hopped out, and the bus continued on its way to Hoopersville.

She walked with quick, light steps across a lawn yellow with dandelions toward a small, white clapboard house of undetermined age. She went around to the back porch.

"Mom!" But there was no answer. It was strange. Usually her mother and two-year-old Kathy came to meet

her when they heard the bus. Meg tugged at the screen door, and it opened with a jerk. Its hinges sagged. Like so many other things around the house, it needed repair, and Dad hadn't gotten around to doing many repairs. He said he'd rather spend his spare time with his family than fixing up a rented house. Meg agreed with him except when she struggled with the screen, or stubbed her toe on her way through a room.

"Mom!" she called from the kitchen, and listened. No reply. Dad had the car, and her mother never took Kathy for a long walk without leaving a note on the kitchen table. All at once Meg heard a whimper. Running into the living room, she found Kathy huddled in the big easy chair, her pale, wispy hair framing a tear-stained face. When she saw Meg, Kathy's whimpers turned to sobs.

"What's the matter, lollipop?" Meg asked, gathering her up. "Where's Mommy?"

Kathy raised her head from Meg's shoulder and turned her flushed face toward the hall. Her blue eyes were wide and frightened, and Meg was suddenly aware that something was horribly wrong. Still holding Kathy, she walked slowly into the hall, trying to calm the dread that was growing within her.

"Mom? Are you there?"

Then she saw. Her mother lay sprawled headfirst down the hall stairs, her neck twisted in a strange sort of way, her cotton skirt tangled up under her thighs. One foot was bare, and the lost shoe lay awkwardly on the step above. Her soft dark hair, not unlike Meg's, lay tumbled over her face. Where her face showed through, the skin was pale as milk.

Meg turned her head away with a sick feeling in her stomach. Her knees had turned to jelly. Her arms tightened around Kathy, who had buried her face in Meg's hair. You poor, poor baby! she thought. Alone . . . for how long? She took one more quick look, then with a shudder fled from the house, across the lawn, and down the blacktop toward their nearest neighbors, the Bradshaws.

Mrs. Bradshaw was in her back yard taking sheets off the clothesline, and Meg ran toward her, stumbling, hugging Kathy to her chest. The older woman raised her hand to wave but, seeing Meg's face, dropped a wet sheet and a handful of clothespins and ran to meet the two girls.

"What's the matter, Meg? What's wrong?"

At first Meg couldn't speak. She was out of breath and numb with shock. Finally, with an effort she said, "It's Mother. She's had a bad fall and . . ." A sob choked her and she couldn't finish.

Mrs. Bradshaw held out her arms to take Kathy. "Merciful heavens! Come into the house and sit down. I'll get you a drink of water." Meg followed her blindly to the door.

"How bad is it, Meg? Should I call a doctor or the ambulance or go over there? What d'you want me t'do?"

"It's no use calling anyone, or doing anything." By now the tears were streaming down Meg's face. "It's no use, Mrs. Bradshaw. My mother's . . . dead!"

The fishing had been good that afternoon, and before long Lloyd and Jamie had caught several nice rockfish. Lloyd looked up from his bobber as a dark cloud came over the sun.

"It's goin' t'rain for sure, Jamie."

"So what? Fish bite best just 'fore rain."

Their father was working on the *Nellie Byrd*, marking

the bad wood that would have to come out and be replaced by new. Now he called them, waving his arms and pointing to the sky. "I'm headin' for home," he hollered. "If you want a ride, you'd better come in. That cloud's got a lotta rain in it!"

The boys pulled in their lines, and Lloyd began rowing for shore. Together they beached the rowboat. Their father met them at the shore end of the dock. They held up their string of fish for him to see, and he nodded his approval.

"You'll make good watermen yet."

At that moment Captain Noah Whitelock came hurrying toward them from his office. When Lloyd saw his face, he knew something was wrong. The captain's usually jovial expression had changed to a frown. His bushy white eyebrows were drawn together, and as he came close Lloyd saw that his bright blue eyes were misty with tears.

"Tyler, I've had a telephone call from Emily Bradshaw. Bad news for you. Awful bad. Come into my office, man." He stood on the dock waiting as Lloyd, Jamie, and their father hurried up to meet him.

A fist of fear had closed around Lloyd's heart. He saw his father's face turn ashen under his tan as they all filed obediently into the boatyard office. Mr. Evans sat heavily in a chair.

"It's Kathy, isn't it?"

"No, it's not Kathy, Tyler. It's your wife Kathleen I'm speakin' of. She fell headlong down the stairs. I'm afraid— She's dead, Tyler."

Lloyd watched the expression on his father's face turn from amazement to horror to grief. Then Mr. Evans buried his face in his hands, and a dry, hard sob wracked

12

his body. "Lord have mercy!" he groaned. "The step. The loose step. It's my doin' she's dead!"

"It was an accident, Tyler. Don't go layin' a whole bunch of guilt on yourself. Look, I'll just go get you a drop of somethin' t'steady you. Then I'll drive you and the boys home."

Filled with pity for his father, Lloyd put his arm awkwardly across his shoulders. He wished he knew some better way of comforting him. Jamie simply sat down on the floor, hugged his father's knees, and cried.

2

RELATIVES CAME from some distance for the funeral on Saturday afternoon. Grandpa and Grandma Venable, Mom's parents, were there, looking frail and old. They had driven down from Salisbury with their daughter, Aunt Lucy, and her husband. Dad's relatives all showed up, too—Aunt Lavinia and her husband, Lester Messick, from Cambridge, Uncles Fred and George Evans and their wives from Smith Island, and Aunt Mary. Meg was especially glad to see her Aunt Mary, who made herself really useful before the funeral instead of bustling and talking like everyone else.

After the simple church service everyone went to the small graveyard nearby. The graves, shallow because of the lowness of the land, were covered by curved concrete slabs. During the burial Meg held Jamie's hand tightly and tried not to look at Lloyd or her father. To keep her composure she focused her attention on trivial things—the hole in the thumb of her white glove, the mole beside Uncle Lester's nose, and Uncle Fred's Adam's apple. The bird on Aunt Lavinia's hat, she decided, wasn't a bird at all but a bunch of feathers tied together. Meg wished that Aunt Lavinia had stayed home. All morning she had been snooping around the house, and in the church she had wedged herself into the small space between Meg and her father.

Back at the house, an ample supper had been prepared by the neighborhood women. Outdoor working men were expected to eat heartily, no matter what the occasion.

"Quite a spread!" Meg heard a voice beside her say.

She turned to see Aunt Mary, who laid her hand gently on Meg's arm. "Meg, listen to me. Don't let them push you around. Our fine relatives, I mean. Stand up for yourself—and your dad."

Before Meg could ask what she meant, Aunt Mary was gone. She and the other relatives from Smith Island had come by boat, and they had to get home before dark. The remaining relatives helped themselves to food, then crowded into the living room. Suddenly, the house seemed to Meg uncomfortably close. She took Kathy's plate and her own and led her out back, where they sat on the edge of the porch, not eating much but watching the shadows creep out of the piney woods behind the house. A ragged flock of ducks wheeled against the saffron sky, heading for the Honga River. From the woods came the mournful cry of doves.

Lloyd slipped out and sat down beside Meg. "They're talking about us," he said. "What's to become of us, where we're to go, and all that."

Meg was astonished. "What do you mean, what's to become of us? We'll stay here with Dad! We're still a family, aren't we? I'll have to learn to do a lot of things Mom always did, but—"

"How about Kathy? She can't stay here alone while we're in school."

Meg hadn't thought of that. A miserable silence fell between sister and brother. At length Lloyd said, "We'd better go back in there and listen. Don't make any noise. They might make us leave." Meg picked up Kathy, and they tiptoed into the kitchen, where they could eavesdrop without being seen.

It was growing dim in the living room, but no one had bothered to turn on lights. Meg and Lloyd could barely make out the figures sitting in the gloom. Neighbors and friends from the village had left, as well as the Smith Islanders. The remaining relatives were just sitting around talking, their empty plates on tables or the floor. Jamie sat at his father's feet, his head turning to look from one relative to another as each spoke. They seemed to be having a heated discussion.

"It seems only right that as Kathleen's mother I should take the children for a spell," Grandma Venable was saying. "It'd only be fittin'. They're good children. Jamie's a mite rambunctious, mebbe. But I'd like t'have them just the same. The schools in Salisbury are good—"

"Not as good as Cambridge," Aunt Lavinia put in. "Besides, Mrs. Venable, your health is . . . well, you're remarkable for your age, but—"

"Lavinia's right, Mother." Grandpa Venable spoke. "Fond as I am of Kathleen's children, it would be too much!"

Grandma Venable shrank back in her chair, defeated.

In the kitchen, Meg and Lloyd looked at each other. Lloyd wiped his brow with his hand in mock relief. The discussion continued.

"I think we should split them up," Aunt Lucy was saying in her brisk, businesslike way. "Then they'd not be a burden to anyone. It'd suit me fine to take Kathy. With Bob and Jeff away at school, I've time on my hands. Alice and Fred said they'd be glad to have the boys. And you, Lavinia, can take Meg. She's old enough to be some help carin' for that big house of yours. What d'you say, Herman?" She turned expectantly to her husband.

Uncle Herman was struggling with a cough. When he could speak he said, "Anything you like, Lucy. It'd mean extra work for you, but if you don't mind that—"

Aunt Lavinia raised her chin and looked down her nose at Aunt Lucy. Her voice was cold, controlled. "As far as help around the house goes, Lucy, we don't need it. We can afford servants. Furthermore, to my way of thinking, Meg's duty lies here. It's up to her to look after her father. I imagine she can learn to cook. Lester and I'll take Kathy. We've not been blessed by children of our own, and we can give her advantages—"

"Lavinia's right," Uncle Lester put in. "We could give Kathy things that—well, that the rest of you would be hard put to—" He cleared his throat. "To tell the truth, you'd be doin' us a favor. My political career is demandin'

17

too much of my time. Havin' Kathy would give Lavinia a new interest, somethin' to occupy her mind."

Aunt Lavinia nodded in smug agreement.

Meg was furious. As she listened, she unconsciously tightened her grip on Kathy, who began to whimper. "Mama! I want my Mama!"

"Let me take her, Meggie," Lloyd whispered. "Come on, Kathy. Let's go for a walk."

"Thanks, Lloyd." Meg watched them go, then turned her attention again to the group in the living room.

Lester's remark had apparently angered Aunt Lucy. She sat rigidly in her chair and said acidly, "Why didn't someone tell me it was Lavinia's state of mind we were concerned with? I thought—"

"Of course, Lucy, we all agree Kathy's welfare is uppermost," Uncle Lester interrupted irritably. "But there's another thing. A child Kathy's age needs young and vigorous parents. Now you and Herman are a little older, and Herman has this cough—"

"Come on, Lester!" Aunt Lucy spat. "You're not all that young and vigorous!"

Meg's ears were roaring, and she was stiff with indignation. She couldn't believe it! They were actually in there fighting over how her own family was going to be divided! She crept closer to the living room door. Her father was speaking.

"Hold on a minute, all of you. Seems you've disposed of my family according to your own lights. Not that you don't mean well. I appreciate that. But I'd like to see the family stay together, if it's any way possible. And I'm sure that's what their mother would have wanted, too. Meg can do an awful lot. She's strong and capable, mature for her age."

"But she's still a child, Tyler!" Aunt Lavinia said. "She's much too young to have the responsibility of raising a family!"

"Lavinia, I guess you'll have to let me be the judge of that. I think we can manage. The boys are most old enough to look after themselves. As for Kathy, perhaps Emily Bradshaw would help."

"Now, Tyler. Be realistic! Emily Bradshaw has four boys of her own! If you could afford to have someone come in, it would be one thing. But you can't. You barely make enough to keep the children clothed and fed, and pay the rent!"

Meg saw her father hang his head, and her heart ached for him. A week ago he would never have let Aunt Lavinia get away with talk like that. Now, it seemed as though all the starch had gone out of him.

"In my opinion," Aunt Lavinia continued, "Noah Whitelock's mighty stingy with his wages. You'd do better in Cambridge. Mark my words!"

"Lavinia, don't you go talking against the captain," Mr. Evans said reproachfully. "I owe him—"

"Be that as it may, there's no question in my mind but what Kathy should come to us. Even if you could afford hired help, how much better for her to be with her aunt than a stranger! Our own dear mama, Tyler, would think well of my bringing up your motherless child."

"You all seem to forget," Aunt Lucy said plaintively, "that I'm Kathleen's sister. Doesn't that mean anything to anyone?"

There was silence in the living room. Meg held her breath. Surely her father would think of something.

He cleared his throat. "You've all had your say. I just don't rightly know for sure what's best. It's good of you,

Lucy, to offer to take Kathy. Mighty good. But I'd like to keep her here. She'd cheer us up, I b'lieve. Soon as school's out, Meg can look after her. Meantime, Lavinia, if you and Lester—"

Meg had heard enough. She tiptoed onto the back porch to look for Lloyd and Kathy. She found them sitting on the steps. Kathy was leaning against her brother, fast asleep.

"What's the verdict?" Lloyd asked.

"Aunt Lavinia's t'have her till school's out."

"Six weeks with Aunt Lavinia! Poor kid!"

Meg scooped her up. Kathy stirred sleepily in her arms.

"You're all right, lollipop," Meg said soothingly. "I'm just taking you up to bed."

3

MEG WAS MISERABLE sitting through an hour of Sunday school the next day. She had to endure a lot of curious, sometimes pitying glances. During the church service that followed, she found some relief in studying her favorite stained glass window. It showed Noah and his wife and a bunch of animals entering the Ark. The animals looked expectant, rather as though they were going on a weekend excursion. She had always thought that the Ark itself vaguely resembled the heavy-timbered workboats on the

Bay, except that the hull was brown rather than white. The waves in the background were pointy and bright blue with little white hooks on top. Behind the waves loomed Mt. Ararat, decidedly purple.

After the service, the Evanses started the two-mile walk home. They could have brought the car, but as a family they had always enjoyed walking together to and from church. Today, however, they were all tired and depressed. Kathy, sitting astride her father's shoulders, looked pale and listless. She hadn't been told yet that Aunt Lavinia and Uncle Lester were coming for her that afternoon. Meg dreaded the moment when the telling could no longer be postponed.

They walked in silence down the blacktop, past a few white frame houses that bordered the churchyard, and came to an area of marsh and woods. The woods were beautiful—covered by a veil of tiny, new-green leaves pierced here and there by the red of swamp maple buds or the dark green of pines. Overhead a pair of buzzards glided lazily, making wide circles in the misty sky.

Suddenly a muskrat ran out of a ditch onto the road in front of them.

"Look at that!" Jamie brightened.

Then up the blacktop they saw a car coming toward them fast. Meg held her breath. The small animal stopped in the middle of the highway, seemingly confused. At the last possible moment he dove into the long marsh grass on the other side of the road. They all heaved a sigh of relief and continued walking.

"Dicky Sawyer sets traps," Jamie said, breaking the silence again.

"At nine years old? I don't believe it." Meg was used to Jamie's tall tales.

"Does, too! Don't he, Lloyd?"

"I guess. He's the type. I don't like trappin', myself. Can't stand to see things hurt." Lloyd was watching the buzzards overhead, trying to imagine how it would be to glide like that, high over the woods, marsh, and water.

"I could do it," Jamie said. "All by myself. I could earn a bunch of money. I wouldn't need your help, Lloyd."

"You'd have to buy traps," Meg said. "And they're expensive."

"Maybe Dicky would lend me some to get started. I could pay him back later. He makes lots of money. I've seen heaps of rat houses on that creek near our house."

"Trappin's over till fall," Lloyd said. "Ended first of March. Game laws."

"Well, then, I'll start next fall. Could I, Dad?"

"Huh? Could you what?"

"Trap rats?"

"Trappin's over for the season."

"That's what Lloyd said. How 'bout next fall?"

"That's a long time off, but I'll think on it."

They were approaching the Fenwick farm, and could see Mr. Fenwick hoeing spring onions in the neat vegetable garden beside his house. His stout wife, still dressed in her Sunday clothes, was sitting on the porch in a wooden swing. Their two little girls, also wearing their good dresses, were playing in the yard.

"Mornin', Joe," Mr. Evans said as they drew even with the garden fence.

"Mornin', Tyler." Mr. Fenwick, a lanky black man, laid down his hoe and walked over to speak to them. "Sorry to hear about your missus. She was a mighty nice lady."

"Thanks, Joe. We appreciate that." Mr. Evans smiled

faintly. "I miss her, Lord knows. But I reckon she's at rest now."

"That's right, man. Amen."

Kathy had gotten down and wandered over to visit the little girls. Meg heard her squeal and turned to see what was the matter. Kathy was beaming, clapping her hands as she stared into a large basket in front of her. The rest of the Evans family gathered around. There, curled up next to their mother, were four gray and white kittens, not much larger than fat mice. They mewed loudly, rubbing blindly against each other and the mama cat, who stared out at the intruders protectively.

The Evanses stayed for a minute to admire the kittens, but when they were ready to go, Kathy set up a howl.

"Mine!" she cried. "My kitties!"

"Well," Mr. Fenwick laughed, "I don't b'lieve their mama's quite ready t'let 'em go yet. But in a few weeks you can sure have one."

After much reassurance on that point, Kathy was ready to leave. She sat happily on her father's shoulder, looking brighter than she had looked for days, waving good-bye to her friends and the kittens.

More than ever, Meg dreaded the coming afternoon.

The Messicks' visit was nearly as bad as Meg had feared. Finally, after all the good-byes had been said, the rest of the family stood watching from the window as Aunt Lavinia and Uncle Lester led Kathy out to their big maroon Buick. The chrome on the car glinted in the sunlight.

"That's some snazzy car!" Lloyd said.

The other members of the family refrained from comment.

"Don't cry, darling," they heard Aunt Lavinia say.

"You'll be fine when you get to Aunt Vinnie's house and see your pretty room and all the lovely new toys. By tomorrow you'll be our Little Miss Sunshine."

"Miss Sunshine! I think I'm gonna be sick. Yuck!" Jamie turned away in disgust.

As she watched the car drive away, Meg realized that her fingernails were pressing so hard into her palm that they hurt. Once they got Kathy back, she promised herself, she'd never let her go again. Ever.

With the passing days Meg and Lloyd worked out ways of managing the house. Lloyd was to wash the dishes and sweep. Jamie had the trash detail. Meg was to take care of the cooking and the laundry. It wasn't easy. Their father, who had never been very good around the house, was now of little practical help. He would go out on the porch after supper and just sit for hours, staring into the woods. Meg, who often saw traces of tears on his cheeks if she went outside to join him, didn't have the heart to press him for help.

Gradually Meg learned about buying groceries and cooking. She hated giving up after-school activities like softball practice and sketching class, but she couldn't help it. There was no way to do everything, and she was determined to take her mother's place as best she could. She would show Aunt Lavinia and the others that she could make a good home for Kathy. She had to.

"And I'm not doing too badly, if I do say so myself," she muttered one evening while peeling potatoes for supper. "I haven't burned the house down yet, and I've only cut myself once this week."

"Need any help?" Lloyd came into the kitchen. "I've finished vacuuming the living room."

He sounded so cheerful that Meg looked up in surprise as she handed him a knife and a potato. "How was school? Something special happen?"

Lloyd adjusted his glasses and began peeling. "We went on a field trip today to Blackwater Wildlife Refuge. It was neat! The ranger—"

Suddenly Jamie exploded through the screen door. "Where're my boots?" he demanded. "I'm goin' to check that creek south of the house for rat houses."

"They're under a pile of dirty clothes by your bed," Meg said, "which, by the way, hasn't been made for days."

"I'll do it later." Jamie pounded up the stairs, down again, and out the door, letting it slam behind him. Things finally seemed to be getting back to normal.

"Now. What were you saying about the ranger?" Meg turned back to Lloyd.

"Oh, he's terrific! His name's Jack Prior, and you wouldn't believe the things he knows about the birds and animals that live on the marsh! All about their breeding habits and what they eat. I'll bet he could identify more'n a hundred kinds of birds. We went up in the observation tower to look out over the marsh. The view was terrific—creeks wandering all over the place, and inlets poking in from the Bay and the Honga River. I spotted an eagle's nest in a dead tree. Mr. Prior let me borrow his binoculars. He said I had the makings of a good ornithologist."

"A what?"

"A bird watcher."

"I wonder if they'd let me come out there sometime and sketch a wild swan."

"Sure. Mr. Prior would. But you'll have to wait until

fall. They nest way up in tundra country. We only saw one today, swimming around all by himself. Mr. Prior said he'd been crippled somehow. They're protected by law, but some hunters try to take them anyhow."

"Why would anyone want to kill anything as beautiful as a wild swan?"

"Oh, they make real great trophies. People stuff 'em and hang 'em on the wall. They're all the more impressive 'cause they're gettin' rare. Some people are beyond belief! Today we saw a poor old duck flying low with an arrow stuck through his behind! How's that for cruelty?"

"Awful!" Meg slapped the lid onto the saucepan full of potatoes.

At that moment there was a knock at the front door. Lloyd went to answer it, then came back to the kitchen looking worried.

"There's a guy out there says he wants to see Dad. I told him Dad was at work. He asked if my . . . my mom was home. You'd better talk to him, Meg."

Meg wiped her hands on the back of her jeans, tucked in her shirt, and followed Lloyd to the front door. The man standing there was wearing a business suit. He had a briefcase in one hand, and with the other he fiddled with the knot of his tie. He glanced at Meg, then said to Lloyd, "I asked to see your mother."

"She's dead," Meg explained matter-of-factly. "You'd better tell me what you want."

The man looked embarrassed. "Well, I was looking for a grown-up person, but—you look like a smart kid, sis. Guess I can give it to you and save myself a lot of trouble. It's a long way down here from Cambridge. Can I come in?"

"All right, mister," Meg said reluctantly. She had a

sinking feeling in her stomach. Something about the man gave her the willies.

He stood in the middle of the living room looking uncomfortable. Meg and Lloyd stared at him in silence. Finally, he opened his briefcase and took out a legal-looking paper.

"Have you kids any idea what this is all about?"

They shook their heads.

"Well, this paper—say, could we sit down? You know, this isn't much fun for me either."

"Okay, mister. You sit down," said Meg. "We'd rather stand."

He perched on the edge of the couch. "This paper is an eviction notice." He held it out to Meg, and she took it. "D'you know what that means?"

"*Eviction?* Does that mean we've got t'get out of the house?" Lloyd gulped.

"I'm afraid so. But not right away. You see, Mrs. Miles —you know who she is, don't you?"

"Yes," Meg said, studying the paper. "She owns this house."

"Good. I'm glad you know about that. Well, Mrs. Miles is moving to California to live with her daughter. She hasn't been well, and her doctor—"

"Get to the point, mister." Meg felt herself growing impatient.

"Well, she decided she'd better sell this house before she moved. You can understand that! We mailed a letter to your father some weeks ago saying the house was for sale. We didn't hear anything at all from him. Mrs. Miles, anxious to be on her way, advertised it at a knock-down price and sold it immediately. The new owners want possession—"

"How long do we have?" Meg asked brusquely.

"Until July first."

When Mr. Evans stepped into the kitchen an hour or so later, he found two worried faces looking at him accusingly. Meg waved the eviction notice in front of him. "Why didn't you do something about the house right away, Dad?"

Mr. Evans took the paper and studied it, bewildered. "You mean the house has been sold?"

"Yes, Dad," Lloyd said evenly," and we've got to get out by the first of July."

"The man said he mailed you a letter several weeks ago," Meg challenged. "There would have been time . . ." She hurried to the stove to pull a smoking pan of bacon off the back burner. "Maybe she'd have sold it to us. You could have asked her!"

"I didn't see as there was any rush." He sat down heavily, hunching his shoulders and putting his hands between his knees. "I figured she'd want too much right off . . . that it'd go more reasonable if it was on the market a spell. That was a few days 'fore your . . . your mother . . ."

"Okay, Dad. I guess your mind's been on other things." Her voice had lost its sharpness. She emptied the bacon onto a platter, then lifted the lid off the potatoes and tested them with a fork.

Lloyd brought a bottle of milk from the refrigerator. "Well, anyway, it looks like we're gonna have t'get out of here."

"Likely I did wrong, Lloyd. I can't seem to put my mind to things the way I should. Without your mother, sometimes it hardly seems worth tryin'."

"I know it's hard, Dad." Meg put the food on the table. "It's hard on all of us. But we've got to keep on from day to day one way or another."

"I'll find a place," her father said. "I'll ask around."

"I hope we're lucky. The first of July will be here 'fore we know it. Now, where's Jamie?"

"Still out on the marsh, I expect," Lloyd said.

"Well, let's start without him. He's old enough to know when it's time for supper." Meg bowed her head, waiting for her father to say grace.

There was a rush of footsteps on the back porch. A boot dropped, then another, and Jamie burst into the kitchen dripping wet. "I slipped and fell in the creek!" he said cheerfully.

THE LAST SATURDAY in May was warm and bright with cotton clouds pasted against a soft blue sky. Meg sat down on the back steps with her cup of morning tea. She was tired of housework and tired of being indoors. She hadn't done any sketching in weeks, and today would be just right for it. Housekeeping was more time-consuming than she'd ever imagined. Something was always breaking or getting dirty. Somebody was always hungry.

"Hi." The screen door slammed behind her and Lloyd

sat down on the steps, a bowl of cereal in his hand. "Sure is a nice day."

"M-mm."

Lloyd slurped cereal. "I bet the crabbing would be good today. Too bad we can't go. Might even find some peelers."

"You think so? They're bringing top prices. I saw a few in the market." Meg looked back at the kitchen and sighed. "I've got mending to do. Jamie's through the knees in his jeans."

The door slammed again and Jamie clumped out, wearing his boots.

"Where d'you think you're goin'?" Lloyd asked.

"Go on back for the trash, Jamie," Meg said. "You forgot to empty it yesterday."

Jamie ignored the order and clambered past them down the steps, then turned to face them in the yard, his jaw set determinedly.

"I'm goin' crabbin'. You guys comin' with me or not? Dicky Sawyer got peelers last week."

"Can't go, Jamie," Lloyd said. "We got work t'do."

"You two aren't any fun anymore." Jamie's lower lip shook a little. "*Mom* never had so much work t'do that she couldn't go crabbin' on a Saturday."

Lloyd and Meg looked at each other.

"You know," Lloyd said, "for once I think small stuff's got something."

All at once Meg made a decision. She stood up, picked up Lloyd's cereal bowl, and balanced her cup and saucer on top of it. "You can cut the grass on Monday after school. Right?"

"Right." Lloyd was on his feet grinning.

"Jamie can sew patches on his jeans himself, patches of his own choosing. Right?"

Now Jamie was grinning, too. "Meggie, I'll take care of the trash soon as we get home. I promise."

"Good. I'll wash up and make sandwiches."

"And I'll go ask Mrs. Bradshaw if we can borrow their skiff." Lloyd was already halfway across the yard as he spoke.

Jamie had disappeared into the shed to get the crab nets and pick up the fishheads he'd been hoarding for bait.

An hour later they were settled in the Bradshaws' skiff. Jamie insisted on first turn rowing. As they moved out into the Honga River, which separates Hooper's Island from the mainland, Lloyd prepared the crabbing lines, stout strings with fishheads attached. Meg sat in the stern with her sketch pad on her knee.

Spelling each other at the oars, the young crabbers progressed slowly up the Honga, skirting the eastern shore of the island. When they came to a likely spot for hard-shell crabs—old dock pilings were considered good —they would tuck in their oars, drop their fishheads into the water, and wait for the crabs to attack the bait. When the lines felt heavy, they would gingerly raise the crabs out of the water and shake them off into a net. Before long they had a bushel basket full of hard-shell. But they hadn't found any peelers, even going in shallow. A peeler, or soft-shell, has shed his shell and is in the process of growing a new one. He stays close to shore, seeking protection among rocks and reeds. Sharp eyes can see his whitish shape moving in the shallow brown water, and a deft movement of a net can capture him before he has a chance to scuttle under a rock.

"Let's look along the shore of Meekins Neck," Lloyd said. "There's a lot of shallow water along that big stretch of marsh."

"That's a heck of a long way!" Jamie's enthusiasm for rowing had diminished noticeably.

"Jamie, you've done your share of rowing. I'll take over when Lloyd gets tired."

Taking turns, Meg and Lloyd rowed the skiff up the river and across the channel which led to the Chesapeake. Finally they reached the marsh on the eastern shore of Meekins Neck.

"Here, take this oar, Meg," Lloyd said. "I'll use the other one to pole along slow and quiet. Maybe that way we won't scare peelers away."

They saw plenty of frogs and turtles but no crabs.

Suddenly, Lloyd nudged Meg. "Look!" he said in a low voice.

"Where?"

Lloyd pointed ahead. About fifty feet back from the water Jamie and Meg saw something sticking up above the marsh grass like a black snake standing on its tail.

"What on earth—?" Jamie asked.

"It's the head of a wild goose," Lloyd answered. "I wonder what he's doing here this time of year."

"Lloyd! I'd love to get a better view. Let's see if we can get any closer," Meg said, leaning out of the boat.

Lloyd grinned. "Sure wouldn't hurt to try."

They beached the skiff, and Lloyd led the way through the grass and scrub of the marsh. He walked cautiously and soundlessly, moving the tall grass as little as possible and making sure of his footing before he shifted his weight from one hummock to the next. The ground grew firmer as they moved away from the water's edge. Soon he dropped to his knees and inched forward on all fours. Jamie and Meg followed. When they were close to the goose, Lloyd stopped still and listened. Then he carefully

parted the tall grass with his hands. Peering through, he saw the goose they'd been stalking . . . and another, a second goose sitting on a mound of sticks and grasses.

"A nest!" Lloyd whispered. His skin prickled with excitement. He'd never been so close to a pair of wild geese or seen so large a bird's nest. He leaned back so that Jamie and Meg could see around him. Then he gestured to them to spread out a little, mouthing the words silently: "Let's stay. Maybe the goose'll move, and we can see if there are any eggs."

They lay on their stomachs in the grass for a long time, watching. But the geese remained as they were—one on the nest, the other standing guard. Jamie was beginning to wriggle uncomfortably. The marsh mosquitoes had found them and were becoming more and more aggressive. Finally even Meg and Lloyd were getting antsy. Just as they were getting ready to give up and retreat to the boat, they became aware of a faint roaring sound, a sound quite out of place in such a remote marshland. Looking at each other questioningly, they rolled over into half-sitting positions, but they couldn't see anything out of the ordinary over the bushes.

"What's that?" Jamie whispered.

Lloyd shrugged and turned back to look at the geese. They, too, had heard the sound. The goose on the nest was making anxious little movements. Beside her, the gander turned his head this way and that as though trying to determine the nature of this threat to his safety.

The sound grew louder and louder. Sometimes it lessened momentarily, but then it increased again, coming on with a rush and a roar. The gander had begun walking nervously up and down. At last his fear got the better of him and he took to his wings, flying low and slow toward the river. The goose stayed on her nest a few more minutes, ruffling her feathers and twisting about. Then she, too, deserted the nest and began waddling awkwardly but rapidly toward the shore. Meg gasped. In the nest were four eggs, real beauties—large, smooth, buff-colored, and perfectly shaped.

Lloyd, watching the goose, noticed that she was dragging a wing. "So that's why they didn't fly north to Canada to nest! The goose is crippled, and the gander wouldn't abandon her. Geese mate for life."

In the meantime Jamie was on his feet, looking over the scrub and bushes for the source of whatever was making all the racket. He pushed through a clump of bushes on a small rise and saw a monstrous bulldozer not a hundred yards away headed in their direction, crunching and flattening everything in its path. Behind it the ground lay naked, scraped bare of every living thing as far as Jamie could see.

"I don't believe it!" Lloyd scrambled up to join Jamie on the rise. They stared amazed at the desolation before them.

"It's tearing up the whole marsh! Why is it doing that?" Jamie finally spoke.

"They must be going to use the land for something— something that doesn't like trees and bushes and marsh grass."

They stood transfixed, watching the bulldozer chew up the ground closer and closer to where they stood. Its heavy caterpillar treads were caked with a tangle of mud and grass. The rest of the machine, except for its enormous steel blade, was painted a glaring yellow. On its high seat sat a red-faced fellow with intense eyes and a hard-set jaw.

"The nest! It's going to run right over the nest!" Jamie shouted to be heard above the racket.

"Not if I can help it!" Lloyd shouted back. "Come on! He'll have to run over us first!" He tore off in the direction of the nest, waving his arms over his head and shouting, "Stop! Stop!" Meg and Jamie ran after him, until they were all in the path of the huge machine.

The bulldozer came on relentlessly. The driver, intent on watching the ground in front of his blade, was unable to see the children or to hear their shouting over the roar of his machine. He got so close they could feel the earth tremble and smell hot oil from the engine. For a moment Meg thought they'd have to run for it, and she put her arm protectively on Jamie's shoulder to push him out of the way if she had to. Suddenly, however, the roar softened to a purr, and the bulldozer came to a grudging halt, its blade just a few feet from where they were standing. The driver leaned forward and stared at them.

"What in tarnation . . . ?" A scowl contorted his face. "Where the devil did you kids come from? I could've run you down!"

Lloyd's knees shook from shock as he walked around to the driver's seat, and his throat hurt from yelling. "Sorry, mister," he said huskily, "but we had to stop you. You see, there's a nest in there." He pointed to the underbrush behind him.

Meg and Jamie, who had come around to stand beside Lloyd, looked up at the driver with hopeful faces. The driver glanced in the direction Lloyd was pointing, shook his head, and reached for the ignition.

"Outta my way! Get on home. You kids got a nerve, I swear. I've gotta finish this strip 'fore quittin' time, and I'm not worryin' about no nest!"

Lloyd took off his glasses, which had been hanging on one ear and the end of his nose, and looked pleadingly up at the driver. "Mister, this isn't any ordinary nest," he explained. "It belongs to some wild geese, and the female's a cripple."

"There are four eggs in it," Meg added, "and they're real beauties! You should see for yourself."

Jamie reached up and touched the man's knee. "Please, mister," he begged.

"It wouldn't take you mor'n a minute," Meg said. "It's not far, just behind that bush."

Lloyd put his glasses back on, and the three of them waited patiently. The driver stared at them, took off his hat and wiped his brow.

"Kids!" He swore disgustedly, putting his hat back on. "All right. All right, you win," he muttered and climbed down reluctantly from his high seat. "Show me the blasted nest."

Lloyd, Meg, and Jamie exchanged a grin and led him through the clump of bushes to the nest. For a minute or two he stood looking at it in silence, the young Evanses anxiously watching his face.

"Where'd the geese go?" the driver asked, finally.

"The goose just now moved off," Lloyd said. "We were watching her when you scared her with the 'dozer. She'll be back. She was dragging a wing, so she can't have gone far. The eggs are still warm, I should think."

The driver looked at his watch. "It's most quittin' time," he said gruffly. "Okay. I'll leave the 'dozer where it is, and talk to the boss on Monday. Mebbe there's some way . . . You sure the goose'll come back?"

"If she's not too frightened, she'll come back," Meg said.

"Yeah, if we get outta here and give her a chance," Lloyd added.

"Okay, kids, I'll see what I can do." The driver's jaw had relaxed, and there were easy lines around his eyes. "You've got a lotta guts to tangle with a bulldozer, and I like that." Turning on his heel, he walked back to his machine.

Meg, Lloyd, and Jamie made their way as quickly and quietly as possible back to their skiff and shoved off. In some river reeds close to the shore Meg thought she spied the goose's head.

That night at supper it was a welcome change for everyone to talk about saving the nest from the bulldozer. All week the mealtime conversation had centered around finding a place to live, and the news was pretty discouraging. Mr. Evans had searched the want ads and asked around for word of rentals or low-priced properties for sale, but so far he hadn't turned up a thing. Rentals were almost nonexistent in the summer season because that was when tourists flocked to the islands. The few houses for sale were either too expensive, too small, or too far from Whitelock's Boatyard.

Mr. Evans enjoyed hearing about the rescue and frowned only once, when Jamie blurted out that the bulldozer had stopped just inches from their toes.

"Ah, Dad, you know how Jamie exaggerates," Lloyd cut in while Meg kicked Jamie under the table.

"Where did you say this nest is?" their father asked when they had finished the story.

"Meekins Neck," Lloyd said. "You know, a mile or so up the river beyond Honga. I'm going up there Monday to see if the goose came back."

"Meekins Neck," Mr. Evans repeated thoughtfully. He was buttering a thick slice of bread. "It just came t'me your Uncle Lester has a piece of property out on Meekins Neck. It's a big piece, a farm, and he uses it for huntin', too. He's got several duck blinds on the river and, if I remember right, a caretaker's cottage. Last time I heard, it was empty."

Meg and Lloyd stared at him as his meaning sank in.

"You mean *live* there? Us, live in the caretaker's cottage?" Meg asked.

"Aye, it's leastwise possible."

"Oh, wow!" Lloyd was already daydreaming. "Practically *next door* to the wildlife refuge. Boy!"

"And not nearly so far from town as we are now. I could stay after school next fall and take art classes again!" Meg looked around the kitchen, already half-planning the packing. Then she frowned. "Dad, d'you really think Uncle Lester would let us have the cottage? Sometimes I get the feeling he—well, doesn't really like us very much."

"He likes Kathy all right." Jamie grimaced. "Old Aunt Lavinia—"

"That's enough, son." Mr. Evans lowered his voice and continued. "Can't say for sure, but it seems to me that Lester might go for the idea of havin' somebody livin' on the place t'look after things. I could fix up the cottage, look after his duck blinds for him, look out for trespassers—that sort of thing."

"Well, at least you could ask. In fact, you could talk to him about it when we go for Kathy." All at once Meg put her fork down and sat up taller in her chair, her eyes shining. "D'you all realize that's only a week away? In *one more week* we'll have the family together again!"

5

LAVINIA MESSICK stood looking anxiously down at Kathy, who was napping on the small bed in the room that had been fixed for her. She lay on her side, her pale hair in wisps around her ear and her lashes lying dark against her pink cheek. Under her chin she held the small blanket she'd brought from home. It was dingy and frayed, but Lavinia had been unable to get it away from her, even for washing.

Aunt Lavinia felt anxious but not defeated as she

thought about her brother coming that afternoon, expecting to take Kathy back to Hooper's Island. There must be some way to keep Kathy. It had been wonderful having her stay with them. She was a lovely child, no trouble to speak of, and if she grew tiresome, Rose the maid could always take over. It had been delightful yesterday, when her bridge group met, to introduce Kathy and hear her friends admire the child. Mabel Strauss had brought Kathy a beautiful picture book, and they had all said how good it was of her, Lavinia, to care for her widowed brother's baby. There must be a way!

She bent over and looked at Kathy more closely. It seemed to her that Kathy's cheek was unnaturally flushed. Perhaps, if she were ill . . . Lavinia laid her hand on Kathy's forehead, and Kathy opened her eyes.

"Mama come? Daddy come?"

Lavinia pressed her lips more tightly together. It was the same question Kathy'd asked every day since she'd been with them. One would think, after all they'd done for her, the child would talk less of Mama and Daddy and show more affection for her! It just wasn't fair. Tyler was simply being selfish, to take Kathy away so soon. She would talk to him. If he insisted on being foolish, she would just have to . . . take more drastic measures and get her back. She didn't know quite what the measures would be yet, but she would think of something.

"Go back to sleep, darling," she said, smoothing Kathy's hair. "Aunt Vinny's here."

Meg had put on her best dress to go to Cambridge. Standing in front of her mirror, she twisted her hair into a soft coil on top of her head to make herself look older.

Her fingers trembled with excitement as she put in the pins. When her father drove up from the boatyard, she was waiting in front of the house.

"Let's go, Dad!" she said.

"I'll just wash up and change my clothes."

"Oh, Dad, don't let's take time for that! You look fine."

He smiled indulgently. "You're mighty anxious t'see Kathy, aren't you? Well, I am, too. I reckon Lavinia can take me as I am." He opened the car door. "Jump in."

"Hey, wait for me!" Lloyd ran out of the house, followed by Jamie. "I want t'go with you far as Meekins Neck."

I might have known Lloyd would want to see his geese today, Meg thought. She'd been planning on his staying with Jamie.

"You going, too, Jamie?"

"Nope, I'm goin' fishin'."

"Why don't you go with Lloyd? I don't like the idea of leaving you alone."

Jamie shook his head stubbornly.

Their father spoke up. "How about comin' with us to Cambridge, son?"

"No way! The shad are runnin' and I'm not goin' anywhere, much less to Aunt Lavinia's. Please, Dad! I'm just goin' fishin' off the bridge."

"All right, I reckon. But hang around, Jamie, d'you hear? Stay on the bridge or near the house."

"Okay. Sure. 'Bye!" Jamie yelled as he ran to get his gear.

Lloyd got in the Chevy and slammed the door, and they were finally underway. Meg felt uneasy about leaving Jamie alone, but reassured herself. After all, he went off alone every day on some adventure or other.

Aunt Lavinia's house was impressive—a three-story, red brick structure surrounded by a high, wrought-iron fence.

"Sure is quiet around here." Meg looked around as her father parked the car at the curb. They walked through the ornate gate up to the entrance, which was flanked by stone lions. The windows were heavily draped.

"Creepy."

"Lavinia always did go in for show," Mr. Evans said, ringing the doorbell. They stood listening to its sound echoing through the high-ceilinged rooms within.

After a minute a woman servant half-opened the door. She looked at Mr. Evans suspiciously. "I expect you're here to fix the washer. You best go 'round back."

At that moment Aunt Lavinia came running down the stairs. "It's all right, Rose," she said. "That's my brother."

The woman muttered apologetically and hurried away. Aunt Lavinia opened the door wider. "Why, hello, Meg. I didn't realize you were coming. Tyler, I'm sorry about Rose. Her manners leave something to be desired. Come on in."

"My clothes do, too, Vinny. I didn't take time to change."

"Hello, Aunt Lavinia." Meg followed her father into the hall. Her eyes traveled up the staircase. She guessed Kathy might well be up there, but her aunt led them into the living room, where they sat facing each other on stiff chairs.

"You're looking well, Vinny," Mr. Evans said.

"Wish I could say the same about you, Tyler! You're thin, and your color's none too good. Is Meg taking proper care of you?"

"She's doin' mighty well, considerin'. All of us are

sufferin' under a heavy loss." He bowed his head and looked down at his hands clasped together in his lap. "I keep lookin' to the Lord to ease my pain. So far, He hasn't heard me. He will, though. I don't doubt He will."

There was an uncomfortable silence. At last Meg blurted out, "Where's Kathy, Aunt Lavinia?"

"She's upstairs napping, dear. But let's don't disturb her now. When I put her down for her nap, I thought she felt a bit feverish . . . most likely only a cold, but one can't be too careful."

"We can keep her warm in the car, Aunt Lavinia," Meg put in, "and see that she gets to bed as soon as we're home. Perhaps I could get her ready, if that's all right with you, while Dad . . . Dad has something he wants to talk to Uncle Lester about."

"Lester's in the den talking politics with some of his friends, Tyler. What did you have in mind?"

"The house's been sold, Vinny, and we have t'find another place t'live."

"The house sold! When did that happen? How long do you have?"

"We have to vacate July first. I was thinkin' that, if Lester could spare us a few minutes, I'd like t'talk to him about a plan I had."

"I'll go get Kathy, Dad." Meg stood up.

"Now, just a minute!" Aunt Lavinia held up her hand. "Before anyone does anything, I think we should discuss seriously the whole matter of Kathy's future."

Meg sat down reluctantly on the edge of her chair.

Aunt Lavinia looked severely at her brother. "Tyler, I firmly believe you should leave Kathy here." She raised her hand to silence their protests. "Now hear me out,

46

brother. You owe me that. I've thought this over very carefully. It's Kathy's welfare I'm thinking of." Mr. Evans sat back in his seat as Lavinia continued. "Les and I are fond of Kathy and can give her every advantage. She has her own room and my undivided attention, and in the years to come . . . I know how much you'd like to take her with you, Tyler, but we have to think of her security and well-being, don't we? Especially since your house's sold. Think, man! It's only sensible to leave her here. Finding another place won't be easy!"

"I don't know what I should do, Lavinia," Mr. Evans said unhappily. "You put it like that, and it seems reasonable. We miss her real bad, but mebbe we're thinkin' too much of our own feelin's. I don't rightly know what's best."

"I do!" Meg was on her feet again, facing her aunt. "Kathy belongs with us! Being with her family is more important for Kathy than having her own room or—or 'advantages.' We'll find a place to live somehow, and no matter where it is, we want Kathy with us!"

Aunt Lavinia's eyebrows shot up to her hairline. "Why, Meg! I'm surprised! What a way t'talk! My dear, I had no idea—" She forced a smile and went on smoothly. "That's all right, dear. You're too young to be objective enough to take the long view. Tyler, what Kathy needs is a mature person to care for her, not a headstrong teen-ager!"

Mr. Evans stood up. "Vinny, you're not being fair. I reckon we've had enough talk for now. It's time we saw Kathy. If you'll lead the way, we'll follow."

Grudgingly, Aunt Lavinia climbed the stairs, her brother and Meg close behind. She paused in front of a bedroom door, put her finger to her lips, and looked warningly at the other two. Opening the door with care, she was surprised to find Kathy standing just inside, her blanket trailing behind her. She didn't look sick at all.

When Kathy saw her father she gave a glad cry and ran to him. He picked her up and held her close.

"We're goin' home now, Kathy," he said, his eyes moist. "Meg, gather up her things. I'll just go down and have a word with your uncle. Lavinia, I'm sorry to disappoint you. I'm grateful for all you've done. But Meg's right. She belongs with us." Carrying Kathy, he went downstairs with Lavinia following him, protesting.

Meg made quick work of packing Kathy's clothes, then went downstairs herself and made her way to Uncle Lester's den. Her father, still holding Kathy, stood in the doorway talking to him. He was saying, "If we could rent it, Les, we'd keep an eye on the place for you and see t'any repairs."

"Sorry, Tyler, The answer's no. I've got people coming down from Baltimore all the time to hunt. They don't stay long, but I've got to have room for them." Seeing Meg he said, "Why, hello there, young lady!"

"Hello, Uncle Lester. Dad, are you ready to go?"

Uncle Lester chucked Kathy under the chin. "So you're leaving us, little girl! I figured your Aunt Lavinia'd find a way to keep you."

Kathy hid her head on her father's shoulder.

"About the cottage, Les." Mr. Evans made one more effort. "With a little notice, mebbe we could move out for a few days, if you needed the space."

"No, Tyler, it wouldn't work. Sorry."

Meg's heart sank. She could tell there was no use pleading with Uncle Lester. He didn't much seem to want them on his Meekins Neck farm, and that was that.

48

"Well, I figured there was no harm in askin'," Meg heard her father say, discouragement plain in his voice.

"No harm in askin'," Uncle Lester repeated cheerfully. He clapped his brother-in-law on the shoulder.

Meg hardly heard the end of the conversation. She was staring at the large white bird mounted above the fireplace, its wings spread wide over the dark paneling. The neck curved upward in a graceful arch, ending in a small neat head with black daggers pointing toward the orange bill. It was a wild swan. How typical of Uncle Lester, she thought. He not only kills illegal game; he stuffs it and has it mounted.

Aunt Lavinia stood tight-lipped at the door to say good-bye, dabbing at her eyes with a white handkerchief and sniffing. Meg was surprised to find she felt sorry for her. "Good-bye, Aunt Lavinia," she said. "Kathy'll be fine. You'll see."

"Come and see us any time, Vinny," Mr. Evans said, "and thanks for your help."

Meg was quiet as they started the drive back to Hooper's. It was sobering to have their hopes for the caretaker's cottage dashed. Kathy, on the other hand, babbled happily about everything she saw—trucks on the highway, grazing cows in a pasture, a barking dog that ran alongside the car. Meg found the weight of Kathy on her lap comforting.

Suddenly Kathy asked, "Mama home?"

Meg was taken by surprise. "Oh, no, lollipop. Mama—Mama's gone away. She's—"

"She's in heaven, Kathy," their father said.

"What's heaven?"

"That's where you'll go when you die," he replied. "It's a nice place."

Kathy's eyes widened. "Don't want t'die!"

Meg hugged her. "No, lollipop, not for a long, long time. Kathy, look at all those blackbirds circling in the field. So many birdies!"

"It's goin' to rain . . . rain hard," Mr. Evans said. "Circlin' birds are a sign. Look at those clouds!"

Meg saw heavy dark clouds gathering in the west and a flicker of lightning. A gust of wind rattled the windows of the old Chevy, and there was a rumble of distant thunder. Meg didn't like storms, but the other thing worried her more. "Dad, what'll we do now about a place to live?"

"Just start askin' and lookin' all over again." He patted her hand. "We'll find something, Meg. Have faith."

But for her, faith was lacking. Instead, she had a clear vision of all their worldly goods piled in front of the house at the edge of the blacktop while they stood helplessly by, watching as the new people moved in.

The rain started as they left Golden Hill, and by the time they got to Tar Bay, it was coming down in a solid gray sheet. It hit hard, drumming noisily on the roof of the car, leaking in around the doors, and cascading down the windshield. Meg and Kathy were both a little scared, and Mr. Evans drove slowly with his face close to the glass, straining to see the road.

"Hope Lloyd got home all right!" Meg said.

"Reckon he did. He's not wantin' for caution."

They reached the bridge, and their tires bumped endlessly over the loose planks as the wind buffeted them. At last they came to the end, the car skidded onto the rainslick blacktop, and in another few minutes they were home.

They sat in the car hoping the downpour would let up,

so they could make a dash for the house without getting drenched. Then the front door was flung open, and Lloyd stood in the opening. "Jamie hasn't come home!" he shouted above the noise of the pelting rain. "He must be somewhere out on the marsh!"

Meg and her father stared at each other across the seat. Then Mr. Evans grabbed Kathy, and they ran across the wet, muddy grass, up the front steps, and into the house.

"Jamie must be somewhere out on the marsh," Lloyd repeated as they stood dripping in the hall. "I found his fishing rod and bait bucket by the side of the blacktop. I was just fixin' to go out after him."

Mr. Evans put Kathy down and started for the back porch. "I'll get my boots," he said. "Meg, dry Kathy off. Lloyd, get the flashlight. Get your coat, too. I may need your help."

In a minute they were ready, and Meg watched anxiously through a streaming window as her father and Lloyd disappeared down the blacktop. Lightning flashed, illuminating their figures, followed by thunder and still deeper gloom. Meg knew well that storms are dangerous on the marsh. There is nothing to break the force of the wind, no shelter from the rain. The land is so low that creeks spill over their banks, and finding solid footing in the resulting floods becomes almost impossible. Poor Jamie! she thought. I hope Dad finds him soon.

Leaving the window, the girls went into the kitchen and dried off. Then Meg made supper. But before Kathy finished her pudding, her head was nodding. Meg led her upstairs, ran warm water into the bathtub, and plopped her in. Kathy slid around on her stomach and kicked her feet, pretending to swim. Then she sat up and tried to capture the soap, but it jumped out of her hands like a live thing. She giggled. Meg joined in the fun, not letting her own worry about Jamie show. Homecoming was for warm feelings and laughter.

Finally Meg lathered Kathy slippery, let her splash one more time to rinse, and scooped her out of the tub. Wrapping her in a big bath towel, Meg carried her to her own big bed, where she lay looking like a plump, terry-cloth sausage. Meg took hold of the towel and rolled her out, turning her over and over. Kathy laughed delightedly.

"Do it again, Meggie! Do it again!"

They played the game until Meg's arms were tired. Then she put Kathy's pajamas on, gave her her blanket, and sat down beside her on the edge of the bed.

"Kathy, how'd you like living at Aunt Vinny's?"

"She gave me presents. But she didn't play good like you do, and her mouth is funny. Then Rose took me. Rose has a hurt in her back. No more Aunt Vinny's!"

"All right. No more Aunt Vinny's."

"I want t'be here with you'n Daddy."

"Good. We want you here, too." Meg buried her nose in the nape of Kathy's neck, relishing the sweet, little-girl smell of her. Kathy put her arms around Meg, holding her tight. "Don't go 'way, Meggie! Dark'll get in my eyes."

"The dark can't hurt you."

"Stay here, Meggie."

"Well, for just a minute. But you must lie still and go to sleep."

Gradually Kathy let go of Meg. "Is Jamie gone away like Mama?" she asked sleepily.

"No, of course not. Daddy and Lloyd will find him and bring him home."

Kathy began to breathe deeply. Meg sat there for a few minutes after she was sure Kathy was asleep. No more Aunt Vinny's, she thought. I'll do whatever I have to. I'll find a way. She picked Kathy up carefully and laid her in her crib. Going to the window, she searched the blacktop stretching away toward Hoopersville, hoping for some sign of her father and the boys.

6

JAMIE'S FISHING had not gone well that afternoon. He had stood on the bridge for an hour or more, patiently trying his luck in various spots. He had had several bites, but each time the fish had cleaned his hook and gotten away. Disgusted, he finally pulled in his line, picked up his bait bucket, and started for home.

As Jamie rounded a curve in the blacktop, he saw a dingy car parked on the shoulder of the road near the creek that skirted the highway on the Honga side. A roughly dressed man in wading boots was walking fast along the bank of the creek toward the car. He was carrying a burlap sack with something obviously heavy in it, and as he neared the car he looked furtively around. Seeing Jamie, he hastened his pace—opened the trunk, threw the sack in, and drove off.

"A poacher! And I'll bet anything he's got that bag full of muskrats." Jamie ran to the spot where the car had been parked and spotted the footprints made in the mud by the man's wading boots. He just had to go and find out what that man had been up to. Leaving his fishing rod and bait bucket by the side of the blacktop, he followed the footprints. He was mainly on the lookout for a heavy stake in the water near the bank such as was used for holding traps. It wasn't until he felt a drop of rain on his cheek that he looked up. Then he saw masses of black clouds flicked by lightning in the west, moving toward him across the sky.

He stopped. He knew he should turn back. The marsh was no place to be in a heavy rainstorm. Then he looked at the continuing footprints. They were hard to resist. He walked fast over the marshy, uneven ground hoping to locate the trap or traps and make it back to the blacktop before the storm broke. All at once he stopped, confused. There were no more footprints. In front of him the creek split and flowed around a small, brush-covered island. The last visible footprint was headed right into the creek, in the direction of the island.

The creek was shallow enough for a man with wading boots to cross without getting wet. It wouldn't be as easy for Jamie. But having come this far, he hated to turn back. Rolling up his jeans, he sloshed across and scrambled up the bank.

By this time it was raining hard. He circled the island,

slipping and sliding on the wet grass. Then he saw what he'd been looking for—a heavy stake driven into the creek bed near the bank. Just beneath the surface of the moving water he caught a glimpse of metal.

Where he stood, the creek had eroded the bank so that it was high above the trap, high and slippery. Holding onto a clump of grass, he let himself down slowly, digging the heels of his sneakers into the mud as best he could and advancing only by inches. Suddenly, the clump of grass came out by the roots, and he slid fast, feet first toward the water. His right foot hit something hard. There was a snap, and the jaws of the trap closed over the toe of his sneaker. He cried out with pain that ran from his foot all the way up his leg and into his back, but only the marsh birds and muskrats were near enough to hear.

For a few minutes he lay on his back in the shallow water, nauseous and faint with pain. Then fear of drowning in the rising creek made him move in spite of the pain. He threw his left leg over his right so that he was lying on his side and clawed his way far enough up the bank to grasp a root that stuck out of the mud above his head. Holding onto the root with both hands, he pulled with all his might, trying to free his foot. It was no good. The trap held him securely. Then he tried to reach down into the water and release the trap, wincing with pain every time he moved. He was in an awkward position, hampered by the rising water. Hard as he tried, his fingers couldn't make the stiff mechanism work. He couldn't budge the stake, either. At last he lay back on the bank exhausted. He closed his eyes, and after a while a sort of numbness dulled the pain in his foot and crept into his brain. The water in the creek was rising rapidly.

Lloyd and his father stood at the edge of the road where Lloyd had found Jamie's fishing rod and bait bucket. Mr. Evans played the beam of his flashlight up and down the area, looking for some sign to show which way Jamie had gone. The rain had washed out all traces of footprints, but the poacher's tire tracks were still faintly visible on the soft shoulder of the road.

"You figure he went off in this fella's car?" Mr. Evans' face was lined with worry.

"No. It'd be more like Jamie to head off across the marsh to see what this man had been up to."

"Likely you're right."

Following this hunch, they left the blacktop and trudged out along the bank of the creek. It was rough going. Lloyd was wearing a jacket with a hood tied around his face, but it was raining so hard that water managed to get in anyway and trickle down inside. His glasses were giving him trouble, too. The water on them made it hard for him to see. He took them off, reached under his jacket for the edge of his shirt, and dried them. When he put them on again, he pulled his hood farther forward as a shield. He had to run to catch up with his father.

"Dad, why d'you suppose he didn't just come home when the storm blew up?"

"Mebbe he was lookin' for muskrats and the rain caught him unawares. He might be marooned somewhere by high water. Or lost."

Lloyd looked around. The marsh did look very different in the rain. All familiar landmarks were transformed by the gloom, and the creeks were so swollen and spread out they didn't look natural. The creek they were following was twice its normal size. They slogged along its

57

bank, Mr. Evans flashing his light in all directions, both of them looking for a small figure lost and wandering aimlessly or a bunched-up shape on the ground that might be a small boy hurt or afraid to move because of the rising water.

Mr. Evans stopped and shouted, "Jamie! Oh, Jamie!" They waited, listening. But there was no sound other than that made by the rain and the swiftly flowing creek.

They plodded on, slipping and sliding on the rain-slick grass, calling now and then and looking all around. Sometimes the lightning flashed, giving them a wider view than the flashlight's beam provided. But still they could see no sign of Jamie. They kept on and on, searching and calling, growing more afraid for him as they went deeper into the marsh.

"He could've slipped and fallen into the creek," Lloyd said, his eyes drawn to the swollen stream. "He can swim when things are normal, but that water's movin' at an awful rate!"

"Pray God he's not in the water!"

A sudden flash of lightning showed them the black water of the Honga River close by. They had come a long way.

"We'd better turn back," Mr. Evans said. "He might've branched off anywhere between here and the road and struck out across the marsh. Sooner we get back and start over, the better!" He turned on his heel and headed back the way they'd come.

The lightning flashed again, lighting up the whole sky and the marsh as well, clear to the piney woods. Lloyd stood awestruck, half scared, half admiring the wild beauty of marsh, river, and sky. Then, in the last second before the brightness faded, he saw something so strange and out of place in the marsh, something so extraordinary that it made him gasp. Then it was dark again, and the thunder roared.

His father looked back. "Come on, boy! What ails you?"

"I thought I saw—" Lloyd suddenly felt so uncertain of what he'd seen he said no more.

"Did you see aught of Jamie?"

"No."

"Well, come along then. At the rate the water's risin', there's no time to lose!"

They decided to go back along the opposite bank in case they'd missed him. They crossed the creek, struggling to keep their footing against the current even in the shallow place they'd chosen. Then they started back toward the road. The creek looped and looped, so sometimes after a five-minute walk they were only yards from where they'd been before. Again and again Mr. Evans called, but there was no answer. Lloyd was soaked, and his legs were beginning to ache with tiredness. Suddenly, he grabbed his father's arm. "Dad! I think I heard something!"

They stopped and listened. But all they heard was the pelting rain and the rushing water in the creek.

"Let's call again, Dad. Maybe this time he'll hear us."

"Jam—ee! Jam—ee!" they shouted together, and again listened. No answer.

At last the storm was letting up. The rain had gentled, and the sky lightened a bit. Once more they called, and very faintly they heard something—something that might be the high-pitched cry of a water bird, or possibly a small boy's cry for help. They hurried on, called again, and this time there was an answering cry. "Help! Help!

Please, help me!" The cry came in high, distressed tones, clearly Jamie's.

It seemed to come from the other side of the creek. Mr. Evans turned his light in that direction, but all they saw was the fast-flowing water loaded with debris and the high, muddy bank of an island midstream.

"He's over there," Lloyd said with conviction. "I'm sure of it. Jamie, where are you?" he called.

"Here! On the . . . the bank. On the island."

Mr. Evans took several strides forward and again played the beam of his light carefully up and down the island's bank. Then they saw him, a muddy lump half-covered by water. His hands, wrapped around a root sticking out of the bank, showed whitely against the dark earth.

"Take it easy, Jamie! I'm comin'," Mr. Evans called.

"Hurry, Dad! It's—my foot's caught!"

"Lloyd, keep the light trained on him. I want a stout branch to use as a staff." Quickly finding what he wanted and using it to steady himself, he waded into the swollen creek. He took one step forward, then another. The water rose over his boots, his thighs, high as his waist. Then he was midstream. Step by step he kept going until he stood beside the poacher's trap just below Jamie. Jamie was whimpering with pain.

"Hold on, son," he said. "I'll have you out of here in a jiffy!" Standing legs apart to keep his balance against the tug of the water, he felt for the trap, found the release mechanism, and sprung it. He picked Jamie off the bank and loaded him onto his back. Then, holding Jamie's arms around his neck with one hand and his staff with the other, he waded back across the creek. Gaining the bank, he let Jamie slide off onto the grass, where he sat, a miserable heap shaking with cold.

Mr. Evans took off his jacket and wrapped it around Jamie, then emptied his boots. "Thank the good Lord we found you when we did! The water's not done risin' yet! If it'd come higher 'fore we found you, or if you'd let go of that root, you'd've drowned!"

"How come you were such a dummy . . . gettin' caught out this way in a storm?" Lloyd asked. He was tired and wet, cross because he'd been so scared for Jamie.

Jamie winced as his father knelt to examine his foot. "I wasn't being a dummy. I saw a guy, and a car, and I was lookin' for his traps."

"Well, you sure found one!"

"I slipped!"

"How'd you know he'd set traps?"

Jamie looked at Lloyd in scorn. "What else'd he be doing comin' out of the marsh carryin' a heavy burlap bag?"

"Well, you're alive, and I reckon you've learned a lesson or two," Mr. Evans said. "Your foot doesn't look too bad. Can you walk?"

"I'll try."

They helped him to his feet, but the moment he put weight on his injured foot the pain made him cry out. "Ouch! That hurts like everything!"

So his father hoisted him onto his back again, and they started home.

"That trap oughta be removed," Mr. Evans said as he trudged along, bending a little under Jamie's weight. " 'Gainst the law!"

"Don't 'spose you saw the license number, Jamie," Lloyd said.

"No. But I think I'd know the car."

"Likely that's not good enough," his father said.

By the time they reached the blacktop, the storm was over. The clouds had lifted, and they could see the western shore of the Chesapeake, a faint, fuzzy line separating gray water and brightening sky.

"Look at that!" Lloyd exclaimed as they climbed up the bank to the road.

Beneath the clouds a scarlet ribbon had been stretched across the sky by the setting sun.

Meg was waiting in the door of the house when they came across the lawn. She'd seen them coming. She ran out to meet them and threw her arms, near as she could, around both Jamie and her father.

"Jamie! Jamie! Are you all right?" She wiped the back of her hand across a damp place on her cheek.

Mr. Evans unloaded Jamie from his back. "I reckon he'll recover in no time flat. He has a hurt foot. That's all."

"Well, there's hot soup on the stove."

After they'd had Meg's soup, Mr. Evans drove to Cambridge for the second time that day to take Jamie to the hospital. Though his foot was badly bruised, only his big toe was broken. The doctor said it would be sore and swollen for several weeks but would mend itself.

It was past ten by the time Jamie and his father returned home. Jamie was put to bed with aspirin, and Meg arranged pillows to keep the weight of the bedding off his foot. Then they all went to bed, relieved and exhausted. Meg lay awake for a moment, thinking. It was a good feeling to have Kathy sleeping soundly in her own crib again. And Jamie had not drowned. He, too, was back home. The problem of finding a house seemed insignificant in comparison. Thankfully, she drifted off to sleep.

In the room he shared with Jamie, Lloyd, too, was thinking—thinking of what he'd seen out on the marsh in the flash of lightning over the Honga. He saw the scene again in his mind's eye—two ghostly poles tall and straight in the lightning's glare. They were taller than most trees. They could've been dead trees with the bark fallen away. But trees that size didn't usually grow in the marsh. Maybe his eyes had been playing tricks on him. But if that was it, it was some trick! He could still see them plain as plain, standing incongruously against the dark mass of the piney woods, out where no poles had a right to be. He knew there was a deep creek near the piney woods just beyond the point, a creek that came in only a short way from the Honga. Could they be—? All he knew for certain was that in the morning he'd have to find out about those poles. At last, he went to sleep.

7

L LOYD HEARD a cardinal whistling in the woods, *ch-e-e . . . chup chup chup*. He opened his eyes. The windows were turning gray. Across the room Jamie lay still sleeping.

Lloyd slipped quietly out of bed, plucked his shirt and jeans from a chair, and tiptoed out into the hall, closing the door carefully behind him. He put on his clothes and started down the stairs. The loose step had been fixed, but it still squeaked. When he put his weight on it, he heard his father cough, then mutter, "Kathleen? That you, Kathleen?"

Poor Dad, Lloyd thought, he's dreaming.

The family was used to Lloyd's early morning rambles. However, he left a note for Meg on the kitchen table. Then he went out on the back porch and pulled on his boots.

It was going to be a fine day. The sky was still gray, but there were no clouds. The breeze had the soft touch of summer, and birds were singing in the woods. He walked along the blacktop until he came to the first creek flowing off toward the Honga, the one he and his father had followed the evening before. There might be a shorter route. He could, perhaps, leave the blacktop sooner, even cut through the piney woods. But he felt the only way to make sure about the two tall poles was to retrace their steps.

The marsh had already recovered from the storm. The water had gone down, and the mud and grass were drying rapidly. The air was cooler than the water, so that mist steamed off it looking soft and mystical. As he trudged along, the sky turned from gray to pale blue. Slowly the woods took on shape and color, seeming to float above the mist. Along the path the blades of grass were beaded with pearls of moisture. All at once the sun pushed up over the horizon, and the moisture turned to diamonds.

With the rising of the sun, ducks along the creek's edge took to the air with a loud quacking, formed themselves into an uneven flock, and wheeled toward the Honga. Lloyd heard a redwing blackbird trilling, then spotted him swaying on a slender reed beside the creek, his song ruffling the tiny feathers at his throat. A minute later he watched a muskrat slip from the bank into the creek, leaving a V of ripples behind him. Near the water,

clumps of marsh marigolds bloomed, and white-veiled beach plums dotted the marsh.

Mist filled the space between Lloyd and the piney woods. He knew that in time the sun would burn it off, but the sun was taking its time, remaining cool and aloof just above the horizon. He stopped, took off his glasses, and wiped them clean. But still he couldn't see through the mist. He was nearly to the river. He'd come a long way, as far as the evening before. If only the mist would lift! He knew it would be folly to strike off blindly across the marsh with no target. Hunger gnawed at his stomach. He thought of his father worrying about his getting back in time for church.

He plodded on a little farther. The creek widened and yellowed in the sun. He turned around. The mist had lifted. Scanning the area, he saw the poles. They stood tall and straight, white against the piney woods, just as he remembered. His heart began to pound with excitement, for he no longer doubted what they were. They were ship's masts. In the lonely marsh far from any large body of water he'd discovered a huge, seemingly abandoned sailing ship.

He ran back along the creek looking for a place to cross. The creek narrowed, and he waded over. He stopped on the other side only long enough to empty the water that had come in over the tops of his boots, then cut straight across the marsh. In places he had to jump from hummock to hummock, but wherever he could, he ran. Then the masts grew taller rapidly. At last, breathing hard, he stood on the bank of the creek where the great ship lay. His eyes swept her from stem to stern, and the size and beauty of her made shivers run up and down his spine.

She was a working sailboat much like Cap'n Noah's *Nellie Byrd*, only her two masts made her a bugeye rather than a skipjack. Like all of her kind she had a shallow draft that made it possible for a waterman to ease her upstream, penetrating the marsh for some distance in spite of her size. Lloyd thought she must be sixty feet at the waterline—more including her bowsprit. Her masts were as tall as her hull was long, raked at a jaunty angle. Lines secured to stakes on the bank moored her fore and aft. But they were no longer needed. She was resting comfortably on the bottom, water flowing around her hull within a foot of her deck.

Her rigging, her sails, all that was salvageable had been removed. Her heavy rail was broken in several places. Some of the posts lay rotting on her deck. The many coats of white paint that had been laid on her were peeling off in large scabs showing dark wood beneath. Altogether she was in a sad state of disrepair, but her condition in no way altered the fact that she was a fine ship, well designed and well built. Her hull, though beamy, swept in a graceful curve from her transom to her lofty bowsprit. She was solidly built of heavy wood put together by expert craftsmen.

Lloyd walked slowly toward her bow to see if she was stove in anywhere. From the creek's bank she looked sound. Standing by her bow, he studied her trailboard, a carved wooden panel that followed the upward surge of her prow. Some of the paint had worn off, but enough remained to brighten the design and make clear the motif. It began with a golden eagle, wings spread, set between two furled flags. Marching toward the bowsprit was a series of shields with red and white vertical stripes sur-

mounted by blue semicircles studded with stars. Midway in the design, spelled out in gilt letters, was the ship's name. She was the *Tessie C. Price*.

Lloyd stood spellbound for a long time. Finally, a great blue heron rose from the opposite side of the creek, bringing him back to reality. Once more he felt his stomach gnawing with hunger. He headed home, going around the head of the creek and jogging through the piney woods.

Meg woke that Sunday morning with disappointment about the caretaker's cottage weighing heavily on her mind. When she found Lloyd's note, it did nothing to lighten her mood. It was a lovely morning, and Lloyd was out there enjoying the fresh air and sunshine, the birds and blooming things, while she was stuck with getting breakfast, cleaning up, and getting everyone ready for church. It didn't seem fair!

Jamie hobbled downstairs, showing considerable pride in his big toe. It was nicely swollen and taking on the color of overripe fruit. He arranged a stool with a cushion on top of it to support his injured foot while he breakfasted.

Meg put bowls of cold cereal on the table and sat down between Kathy and her father. "Dad, what are we going to do now that there's no chance of getting Uncle Lester's place?"

Mr. Evans stirred milk into his tea. "On Monday I'll ask around, put up a notice in the Honga Post Office, mebbe."

"There's less than three weeks before the first of July!"

They heard Lloyd on the porch taking off his boots. He came in with his pant legs wet and caked with mud.

On his face he wore a smear of mud . . . and a grin. "Hi! I'm starved! What's for breakfast?"

Meg was about to say something sharp but changed her mind when she noticed the expression on his face. "Where you been?" she asked curiously.

"For a walk on the marsh."

"You've seen something . . . or found something special. Did you find another nest?"

"No, not a nest."

"Well, what then?"

He fixed himself a bowl of cereal with aggravating deliberateness and sat down at the table, where he took his time about helping himself to milk and sugar.

"Come on, Lloyd. Tell us what you saw." Jamie adjusted his pillow to get more comfortable.

Lloyd looked at Jamie's toe over a heaping spoonful of cereal. "Your toe looks pretty peculiar this morning. That's a weird color!"

Kathy leaned over and touched it with her dripping spoon.

"Ouch!" Jamie yelled. "Cut that out, Kat! It hurts! See, Dad, my toe's really sore—too sore to get a shoe on for church!"

Mr. Evans studied the toe. "It won't matter to the Lord what kind of shoe you wear. I'll cut the toe out of your sneaker for you like the doctor said, and we'll go in the car 'stead of walkin'."

"Dad, d'you think we should report findin' that trap to a game warden since it's out of season?" Lloyd asked.

"Seein' it's sprung, it's doin' no harm at the moment. But if I see the warden I'll mention it."

"Maybe we should see if there are any more traps and bring them in."

"Fact is, I don't like meddlin' with other folks's property."

"Lloyd," Meg broke in, "you haven't told us what you saw out on the marsh. I know from the way you looked when you came in, there was something."

"Pirate treasure!" Jamie said. Kathy's eyes grew wide. "There were pirates here, you know. My teacher said so. They robbed Spanish galleons and then sailed into the Bay. Sometimes they buried treasure. They could've buried some of it 'round here. They were neat! They cut people's throats, and—"

"You certainly know a lot for a little twerp, don't you?"

"Lloyd, tell us what you saw," Meg persisted.

"Let him be, Meg. The boy has a right to keep his own counsel. Now, it's time you all got ready for church."

"Pirates get me?" Kathy asked as Meg helped her down from the table.

"No. There aren't any pirates left. But you know what today is?"

"What?"

"Today is the day we get your kitty cat. Remember? So let's go."

When they stopped at the Fenwicks' on their way home from church, the whole family came out to greet them. Patsy stood shyly by her father, holding a gray and white kitten now grown into a ball of fluff.

"It's real thoughtful of Patsy," Mr. Evans said. "I reckon Kathy wants a kitten 'bout as much as anything there is."

"She's a girl," Patsy said, putting the kitten into Kathy's arms.

Kathy held her new pet tenderly against her cheek,

then put her down on the grass to get a better look at her. The instant Kathy let go, the kitten scampered away and hid under the porch. Kathy ran after her. "Come, kitty, kitty!" she coaxed, bending over to see into the dim space under the porch floor.

"That kitten's a scaredy-cat," Patsy said. "But she's getting braver. Maybe she'll be all the way brave when she's grown up. I'll get her for you."

"'Deed you won't!" Mrs. Fenwick said. "Not in your Sunday dress!"

"I'll get her," Lloyd said. He lay on the ground trying to reach the kitten, who had backed up against the house's foundation. "Come here, Kitty," he pleaded. But she wouldn't come. He wriggled partway under the porch, pushing spider webs away from his face and knocking his glasses askew. Finally, he got a firm hold on the kitten and wriggled out again. The kitten squalled in protest.

"She's a scaredy-cat, all right!" He handed the kitten to Kathy.

The name stuck.

After dinner Meg took Kathy upstairs for her nap, and Scaredy took refuge under Meg's bed. By the time she came down again, Lloyd had done the dishes.

"I'm going back to the marsh. Want to come along?"

"You bet!" Meg's eyes shone with anticipation.

"I'll ask Dad." They found him on the back porch. "Dad, I'm going t'show Meg what I found out in the marsh. Would you like t'come?"

"You kids go ahead. After huntin' for Jamie last night I've had as much of the marsh as I want, time bein'. I'll stay with Kathy."

When Jamie learned where Meg and Lloyd were going, his toe suddenly became less painful. "'Course I'm goin'!

Lloyd, you can make me a crutch. That way I can keep up."

Seeing how determined he was, Lloyd found a stout stick with a fork at one end and wrapped rags around the crotch to make a pad. Then the three of them started out, Lloyd leading the way, Jamie hopping behind with his crutch, and Meg following.

It was cool and still in the piney woods, except for the occasional chattering of a squirrel. Once there was a rustling noise, and Meg caught sight of a white flag, the tail of a deer bounding away. The leaves of maple, sweet gum and oak, hardwoods crowded in among the pines, had pushed all the way out by this time. But they were still the new green of early summer. Sunlight filtered through their branches, making a pleasant dappled pattern on the ground. The smell of the pines scented the air.

They walked a long way through the woods almost to the place where the land poked out into the river, making a witch's finger. Lloyd stopped. "We're almost there," he said, "but it'll be more fun if you do it my way. Jamie, put your hand on my shoulder. Meg, put yours on Jamie. Then close your eyes tight. We're going through a little opening in the trees. I'll tell you when to look, and you'll see . . . well, you'll see what you see."

They moved slowly through the trees, allowing time for Jamie to use his crutch. After a bit Meg was aware of added brightness on her eyelids.

"Open your eyes!" Lloyd said.

Meg's and Jamie's eyelids flew open. Across a narrow strip of marsh they saw the great sailing ship.

"Jumping jellyfish!" Jamie exclaimed. "You found a boat!"

"A ship!" Meg cried. "A beautiful sailing ship! Whose is she, Lloyd?"

"No one's, far as I can tell."

"Let's take a closer look," Jamie said.

"We can see her better on the other side," Lloyd said. "We can go around the head of the creek."

When they came abreast of the old bugeye, Meg and Jamie stared at her unbelieving.

"How d'you 'spose she got way up the creek here, so far away from everything?" Jamie asked.

Lloyd said, "I think some tired old waterman just brought her up the creek to die. Most of these old oyster boats don't make their keep anymore. Probably her owner just got tired of fighting winter weather, power drudgin', and MSX. Yet he couldn't very well leave her to rot in town."

"What's MSX?"

"It's a parasite that thrives on oysters," Lloyd explained. "It's killed 'em off in Tangier Sound altogether!"

Meg was studying her trailboard. "*Tessie C. Price*," she mused. "I like that."

"Let's go on board and see what she's like inside," Jamie said.

"How about your foot?" Meg asked.

"Don't worry. I can hop." He plunged into the creek and in another minute was pulling himself up onto the ship's deck. Lloyd was close behind. Meg hesitated. She didn't like the look of the muddy creek water, and she was certain it would be cold.

"Chicken!" Jamie called. He stood on one foot, dripping and holding onto the rail.

Gritting her teeth, Meg plunged into the water and swam the few strokes necessary to reach the ship. It *was* cold, and she got herself out of the water as fast as possible. The boys were already exploring the deck.

The deck of the *Tessie C. Price* swept wide, flat, and

75

uncluttered from stern to bowsprit. No cockpit broke up the work space; only a doghouse was placed midships to make headroom in the cabin below. Deck boxes in the stern provided some storage. One housed the steering mechanism, at the same time making a seat for the helmsman. Jamie settled himself there and took hold of the wheel, its mahogany spokes worn satin-smooth by the hands of many skippers. He tried to turn it, but the rudder, stuck deep in the mud astern, refused to budge.

"Let's see what's in her cabin."

It took all Meg's and the boys' strength to push back the hatch cover, which was swollen with dampness and tight in its groove. Below the cover was a small door, hinged vertically, which they opened. Then the three young Evanses peered curiously inside. All they saw was water, water on a level with the creek outside.

"Of course she'd be full of water lying here untended all winter," Lloyd said. "Any wooden boat her age would be. It's nothing against her. I checked her hull on both sides. She's not stove in that I can see."

Jamie turned away disappointed. "I guess there's no treasure."

"Of course not, you nerd! She's not a pirate ship. She's nothing but a tired old work boat."

Meg objected. "Not just an old work boat! She's much, much more! She was beautiful once, and still could be. It's a shame to let her go to wrack and ruin!"

They walked toward the bow and found the cover missing entirely from the forward hatch. Jamie kept on going, straddled the bowsprit, and worked his way out to the tip. "Look at me!" he called.

"You're a show-off, Jamie Evans!" Meg said. She and Lloyd stood by the mainmast gazing out over the marsh.

A gentle breeze fanned the grass into ripples, making it into a green and bronze sea. Beyond, they saw the broad blue of the Honga.

"I think she's stupendous!" Meg said. "All she needs is people who care, people who can appreciate what she's been and still is. What if...?"

"What if what?"

"What if *we* were those people? With a little work she could be made into a place for us to live, at least for the summer. We've got to find some place soon. The end of the month is coming fast!"

Lloyd looked at her, his eyes filled with admiration. "It's a great idea—but she'd need a lot of work. We'd have to pump her out, mend her leaks, then put in sleeping bunks."

"And a galley. If Dad was willing he'd know just how to go about it. D'you think he'd be willing?"

"I don't know. It wouldn't hurt to try, I guess." Lloyd's face was beginning to show some doubt. "I think he'd like her. He really goes for old sailboats. We should get him out here and let him see her, then tell him our plan."

"All we'd have to say is, 'Dad, Lloyd found an old bug-eye abandoned in the marsh. Would you like to take a look at her?'"

Lloyd grinned. "It just might work, Meg. I think it's a super plan!"

"Good! We'll try it. Maybe we can get him out here tomorrow. We'd better start back, I guess. It's getting late. Jamie! We're going."

Jamie dropped from the bowsprit with a big splash. A pair of mallards quacked loudly, beat their wings, and ran over the water in front of the bugeye before rising to circle over the children's heads. The great blue heron came flopping upstream, put his long legs down in the shallows on the other side of the creek, and stood looking curiously at the other two-legged creatures that had invaded his territory.

Tessie C. Price. Tessie C. Price. The name kept running through Meg's brain all the way home. Idiot! she said to herself at last. You've let yourself fall in love with an old boat!

8

"TESSIE C. PRICE. Sounds familiar," Mr. Evans said. "Seems like she was out of Cambridge. Used t'be tied up in the center of town."

The young Evanses had wasted no time in telling their father about Lloyd's find. Now, they were on the back porch after supper. Kathy sat on her father's lap, and Meg was at his feet, hugging her knees. Lloyd stood leaning against a post, while Jamie lay on his back, his arms under his head and his sore foot resting on his knee.

"Aye, she was a good old ship," Mr. Evans continued.

"Did a heap of drudgin' in her day. Well built and roomy."

"She still is a good ship, Dad," Lloyd insisted. "We went over her stem t'stern. Her masts and bowsprit are solid, her deck's sound, and the doghouse looks okay. The hatch cover forward is missing, and some of her rail is broke."

"Likely it'd take more work t'make her right for the Bay again than she's worth. I reckon her workin' days are over."

"D'you s'pose anyone's interested in her now, Dad?" Meg turned to look at her father more directly.

"Come t'me the old man owned her left town. Effing, his name was. Jack Effing. He and Barstow and others like him were skippers second to none. They knew how t'find an oyster rock, put a drudge smack on top of it, and depend on wind and sail alone to drag that drudge slow and steady across it, scrapin' the oysters off. But even men like that get old and tired."

"Why d'you s'pose she's up that creek?" Jamie asked.

"Effing couldn't leave her t'fall apart in the center of Cambridge, and she'd be hard t'sell. I s'pose he just took her up that creek and walked away."

"And now, no one cares what happens to her," Meg said.

"Don't reckon they do. What're you gettin' at, Meg?"

"We were wondering if you'd like to go take a look at her."

"I'd not mind doin' that. I'd have an interest in seein' the old bugeye. Tomorrow after work suit you?"

"Oh, sure." Lloyd looked at Meg and winked.

When Mr. Evans drove up to the house late Monday

afternoon, he found his family waiting for him. Meg sat on the top step holding a large covered basket. A big jug stood beside her. Lloyd had propped a plank longer than he was against the house. Jamie and Kathy sat on the bottom step, Jamie holding his crutch and Kathy clutching a brown paper bag. He got out of the car slowly. "What's all this?"

"Nicnic!" Kathy exclaimed, running to him. On the way she dropped her bag. Picking it up she looked inside. "Cookies all broke!" she said sadly.

"That's all right, lollipop," Meg said. "They'll taste just as good. Dad, we thought we'd have a picnic on the deck of the *Tessie C. Price.*"

"You've sure taken a fancy to that old boat! Lloyd, what d'you have in mind for that plank?"

"It's a gangplank. That way everyone won't get wet."

A smile curved the corners of Mr. Evans' thin mouth. "You've thought of everything, haven't you? Well, let's get started. Give me one end of that plank."

Jamie hopped up and with the help of his crutch made good time around the house and into the woods. Kathy and Meg followed with the food, and Lloyd and his father brought up the rear. When they came out of the woods, Mr. Evans rested his end of the plank on the ground and stood looking at the bugeye. "Aye, she's the one I was thinkin' of," he said. "A fine old ship."

Meg and Lloyd exchanged meaningful glances.

"She was built by a man knew his trade, all right. Timber like that's hard to come by nowadays."

They walked around the head of the creek and down the other side. When they were abreast of the *Tessie,* Lloyd waded in with his plank and propped it against the ship's hull. The other end he buried in the mud at the creek's edge. He scarcely had it in place when Jamie hopped up it, his sore toe all but forgotten.

As soon as everyone was safely on deck, Mr. Evans began a careful inspection of the ship. He rapped the planks with his knuckles, listening for the different sound made by rotten wood. Where the paint had peeled off deck or hull, he probed with his pocket knife. But nowhere was the blade easily admitted. He pounded on the doghouse roof and peered down the main hatch, then the forward. He could find no place where the hull was stove in.

"She seems sound enough," he said as they settled on the deck to have their picnic. "Can't see what harm there'd be in your playing around on her, if you like. It's a pleasant location, and a ship has a fascination. I'll nail some boards over that forward hatch. There's enough water inside her hull for Kathy to drown."

They ate their sandwiches of meat and cheese, throwing the crusts to swooping, contesting gulls, who uttered cries of complaint or triumph. There was lemonade to go with the cookies. After the last crumb was gone, the noisy gulls took off, and the Evanses sat quietly watching the sunset, keenly aware of the beauty of creek, marsh, and sky. The afterglow spread a veil of lavender over the sky. In the east a pale star shone through, and a flock of black-crowned night herons flew lazily upstream to feed in the green shallows.

Meg sat beside her father with Kathy's head in her lap. She knew the boys were waiting for her to unfold their plan. "Dad, is there anything new about a place for us to live?" she asked.

"Nothing for certain. I've had a couple of leads, none

too promising. It's a bad time of year. All the summer folk are descendin' on us. In the fall we'd stand a better chance. I'd buy a house if it was priced within reason. I could afford it with help from the bank. So far I haven't heard of anything suitable. Mebbe I should look for work in Cambridge, where housin's not so hard to come by."

Cambridge meant Aunt Vinny's to Kathy. She sat up, her chin quivering.

"Oh, Dad!" Meg exclaimed. "You wouldn't like that."

"No, I wouldn't *like* it, but a man's gotta do what's best for his family."

"I'd hate it!" Jamie said.

"I'm not decided yet," their father continued. "Your Aunt Lavinia telephoned the boatyard this morning. She said she'd heard of a builder needed a carpenter and that she'd her eye on a house, too. Still, I'd not like givin' up boat buildin' and workin' for Cap'n Noah."

Meg took a deep breath. "Dad, how about livin' on the *Tessie*? With a little fixin' up we could live on *her* for the summer."

There was a moment's dead silence. "You mean . . . live on this old boat?" Mr. Evans looked incredulously from one earnest face to another. "Now, see here, the lot of you. That's why that's—"

"A great idea!" Jamie said. "It would be lots of fun livin' on a boat! Like somethin' out of a book!"

"We couldn't live on her the way she is, Dad," Lloyd said. "We know that. We'd have to pump her out, caulk the leaks, put in bunks—"

"And a galley," Meg said. "Don't you see? It would give you a breather, Dad! It would be somewhere to stay till you found something . . . something more suitable.

You don't want to desert Cap'n Noah or give up boat building, if there's any other way!"

Mr. Evans shook his head. "You're daft, the lot o' you!"

"No, we're not, Dad," Jamie insisted. "You said yourself the *Tessie* is a fine old ship! Just imagine how she'd be all fixed up and painted! She'd be fantabulous!"

"A man would need all kinds of power tools and heavy lumber, and she's stuck out here miles from the road. Then there's the weather. It's tolerable this evening, but how would you like it in a storm like we had Saturday night? Not much, I reckon!"

"It wouldn't be all that bad, if she was made tight and secured," Lloyd said. "She'd just float higher with the rising water. We'd batten down the hatches as though we were at sea and—"

Mr. Evans stood up impatiently. He slapped at a mosquito on his neck. "It's just plain foolishness," he said. "I'll not think of settling you kids on an old boat out in the middle of the marsh, and there's an end to it! Come on, Kathy. It's time we headed for home before these mosquitoes eat us alive!"

Late the next afternoon Meg begged a ride from Mrs. Bradshaw, who was going to Honga. She asked to be dropped off at the boatyard. She had a plan, and as she walked down the gravel driveway, she looked around appraisingly.

Whitelock's Boatyard covered more than an acre of land fronting on Tar Bay. There were several buildings—the boathouse for storing small boats, a workshop, and a marine store. The office was in the rear of the store, as were the public showers and lavatories. There were two

docks with slips for tying up and a marine railway for hauling large boats. The main dock had pumps for gasoline and diesel fuel as well.

To one side of the boatyard stood the Whitelocks' house surrounded by green lawn, flowering shrubs, and old trees. A white picket fence separated its lawn from the sparser grass in the boatyard. The house had two stories plus an ample attic under its red roof. Meg had always admired the corner nearest the boatyard, which was shaped like a tower. The sides of the house were shingled and painted white. Apple green shutters hung at its windows. It had two old-fashioned brick chimneys and a broad veranda across the front that gave a fine view of the Bay. On either side of the veranda steps, zinnias, petunias, and marigolds made a bright border. Gingerbread trim hung from the eaves of the house like lace from a white petticoat.

Meg saw a yacht tied at the fuel dock. Her father was tending the gas pump. On the front porch of the store Captain Noah sat entertaining a man and a woman dressed in boating clothes. The captain's old dog, a Chesapeake Bay retriever named Skipper, lay at his feet.

The captain had spent time on the working sailboats as a youth, then become a pilot of a Bay steamer. He had eventually been made captain of one of the big overnight car ferries that made the trip from Baltimore to Norfolk. He was a teller of tales, with bits of yardarm philosophy thrown in, and was considered an eastern shore character by the boating crowd. People sought him out, and he always made the most of an audience.

"Hello, Cap'n Noah," Meg said.

The captain looked away from his audience, his blue eyes twinkling. "Ahoy, there, Meg! How's my girl?"

"Fine, thank you. Cap'n Noah, can I talk with you for a minute?"

"Sure thing, honey. Just make yourself easy while I finish tellin' these folks about life on the old Bay steamers."

Meg had heard the story before, but she sat politely on the porch steps to hear it again.

"You see," the captain said, getting to his feet to demonstrate the action, "the pilothouse on the old steamers was built so's you could hardly see dead ahead. You had t'stick your head out a side window. Knew an old fella, Tilghman was his name, chewed a heap o' tobacco. He had it worked out pretty good. He'd take a good look out his port side, cross over, grabbin' a bunch o' wheel to correct his course as he passed by, and stick his head out the starboard side. He'd take a good look 'round, meanwhile gatherin' his tobacco together, spit neat and clean, then start back across. Baltimore t'Norfolk he got plenty o' exercise, never messed the deck that I heard of, nor run into anything neither. You folks been t'Hooper's before?"

Mr. Evans called from the gas pump, "She's ready t'go!"

Meg walked down the dock with Captain Noah and the people off the yacht. Skipper followed slowly, his legs stiff with age.

"Whare d'you aim to spend the night?" Captain Noah asked the yachtsmen.

"Would you have a suggestion?"

"There's a good place to tie up by the bridge in Honga. Fine seafood restaurant, too."

"Thanks! We'll give it a try."

The yachtsmen cast off. Meg, her father, and Captain Noah stood watching as the yacht moved out under power. Her sails caught the breeze and she heeled over, slipping neatly through the waves that sparkled in the late afternoon sun.

Mr. Evans said, "S'prised t'see you here, Meg."

"Mrs. Bradshaw was going t'Honga and said she'd take me along. I thought you'd not mind my riding home with you. The boys are looking after Kathy."

"I'll be a while. I'm fixin' a leak in a crabber that's promised for tomorrow."

"I don't mind waiting, Dad. I'd like to take another look at the *Nellie Byrd*, now that you've done some work on her."

"Well, all right. I'll get on with my work and give you a call when I'm done." He started off.

"Dad, don't go! I want to talk to both you and Cap'n Noah about the *Tessie*."

Her father turned back.

"The *Tessie*." Captain Noah chuckled. "Your dad told me about her. You kids can have a lot of fun playin' on an old boat. Just be careful—"

"Oh, we weren't thinking of just playing on her." Meg glanced at her father and rushed on. "We want to live on her."

"Live on her! That's a dang fool notion if I ever heard one." Captain Noah looked at Meg as though she'd lost her senses.

Meg began to wish she'd stayed at home. "Dad says the *Tessie*'s in pretty good shape. And we thought, since we're going t'have to move out by July and all . . . it'd just be for a while. She'd be comfortable fixed up. Dad said she was roomy and well built, didn't you, Dad?" She turned to her father with a pleading look.

"I reckon I did."

Captain Noah shook his head. "Meg . . . you can't live

89

on a beat-up old bugeye sittin' out on a creek in the middle of the marsh!"

"Well—" Meg swallowed. "Well, actually, we were thinking of asking you to move her here to the boatyard."

Captain Noah stared at her in silence.

"I guess maybe it wasn't such a good idea after all. But you see, Dad says if we don't find some place to live soon, we'll have to move to Cambridge, where we can get a house cheap. I guess he can find work there. But us kids really don't want to do that."

Nobody said anything. Mr. Evans stared at Meg, stunned by her brashness. Meg looked down at the water. Finally Captain Noah cleared his throat.

"Is the *Tessie* in any condition t'move, Tyler?"

Mr. Evans shrugged. "She might fall apart. She might not. The kids are upset, Noah, 'bout not havin' a place t'live. But we don't want t'put you to any—"

"Hold on there just a minute, Tyler." Captain Noah took off his peaked cap and thoughtfully scratched the bald spot in the middle of his curly white hair. Then he replaced his cap, adjusting it to its usual jaunty angle. He looked across Tar Bay at the buoys that marked the channel leading past Barren Island out onto the Chesapeake. Finally, he spoke. "If we can figger a way t'make her float, we can tow her in here with the *J. P. Leonard*. We could haul her 'round and beach her right there on that low spot next to my picket fence."

"But—"

"We can run water into her galley with a pipe from the store, and you and your family can use the washrooms there. Even workin' just on your own time, Tyler, you could make her livable in a couple o' weeks. What d'you say? Shall we give it a try?"

"I just don't want to—"

"Think of it, man! It'd be real handy for me, real handy t'have you livin' right here in the boatyard, busy time o' the year."

"I don't know. I hadn't thought of it just that way. If you want to take the trouble and would put up with havin' the kids here . . . How 'bout Mis' Whitelock?"

"Look, Tyler. I've known you since you was a boy on Smith Island. You've been a good friend and a good worker for a lot of years. I'll be danged if I'll lose you to some second-rate yard in Cambridge over a place t'live. It won't hurt t'try, right?"

Meg's father grinned. "All right. All right. I shoulda known with the two o' you workin' together on this outlandish scheme I'd not stand a chance."

Meg threw her arms around her father's neck, then the captain's. "Oh, thank you, thank you, Cap'n Noah. Dad, it'll work out real well. You'll see."

"I hope you're right. You'd better not get all het up about it. We haven't even figgered how t'make the *Tessie* float yet."

"You will."

"And takin' care of a family on a boat won't be as easy as in a house."

"I don't care. I'd settle for boatkeepin' instead of house-keepin' any day."

Captain Noah's blue eyes crinkled up with laughter. "I s'pose you think livin' on the old bugeye'll be a lark. Well, mebbe it will be, at that."

"Sure it will, Cap'n Noah. Now, I want t'see your *Nellie Byrd.* Dad says you're going to sail her in the Fourth of July skipjack race."

As she followed Cap'n Noah across the boatyard, Meg

breathed a sigh of relief. Now they wouldn't be put out of the house with no place to go. They wouldn't have to move to Cambridge and be bossed around by Aunt Vinny. If only the *Tessie* would float!

W HEN MR. EVANS broke the news to his other children that he and Captain Noah would attempt to haul the *Tessie C. Price* around to the boatyard, they could scarcely contain their excitement.

Jamie began hopping around the room like a kangaroo, using his crutch to balance. "You mean we're goin' t'live on her after all? Yippee!"

"Whoa there, young man! Reckon your hearin's a bit faulty. I said *attempt!*"

"I've got this feeling," Lloyd said solemnly. "I've got this feeling it's goin' t'work. I wager we'll be livin' on the *Tessie* by the Fourth of July."

"Don't count on it, son. Still, if it's a calm day tomorrow, we'll try haulin' her 'round. The captain and I figger the thing t'do is pump her dry, then lash empty oil drums 'long her sides t'keep her afloat. Cap'n Noah's *J. P. Leonard*, that big diesel-powered fishing boat of his, oughta be able to bring her in."

"Can Scaredy live on the boat, too?" Kathy asked.

" 'Course, silly." Jamie came to a halt in front of her. "That is, if you can get her out from under Meg's bed."

Meg picked Kathy up and twirled her around the room. "We'll all live on the *Tessie*, lollipop, the whole lot of us!"

To everyone's disappointment, dawn brought a blustery wind that whipped Tar Bay into steep little waves. They'd have to wait for a calmer day to fetch the *Tessie*.

With an empty day ahead of him, Lloyd decided to go as far as the boatyard with his dad, then walk the rest of the way to Meekins Neck to see his geese. Meg reluctantly admitted to herself that there was no excuse for delaying longer the business of getting ready to move. It would be a big job. She must sort, pack, and throw away. She must decide what to sell to the new owners and what to send to a second-hand-furniture dealer. Some things, Captain Noah said, could be stored in the loft above the boathouse until they were needed again. Only necessities could be taken aboard the *Tessie C. Price*.

With a sigh Meg mounted the ladder that led through the trapdoor to the attic. Kathy tagged along behind. Meg looked around, and her heart sank. She saw boxes and boxes, some with their contents spilling over their sides.

There were keepsakes of bygone days, early correspondence, old snapshots, baby clothes. Odd bits of furniture were shoved into corners. There was the rocking chair with its cane seat gone that her mother had used to rock them when they were little. There, too, sat a sea chest that had been in the Evans family since the first Evans, Jeremiah, had come from Wales to settle on Smith Island. Now it held the blue willowware china that had belonged to great-grandmother Middleton.

Kathleen Evans had put away the family's winter clothes only a few days before her fatal fall. Meg saw her mother's old coat hanging in a wardrobe with some other things. It was bright red with a black fox collar. Meg remembered it as being decidedly becoming, but it was of no use to the family now. She took it from its hanger. All at once a big lump came into her throat, and she sank to the floor, her face buried in the old coat, her tears wetting its fur.

In another part of the attic Kathy was busy, too. "Look at me, Meggie!" she called.

Meg looked up. Kathy had found a captain's peaked cap many sizes too large and plopped it on her head. It covered her ears and very nearly her eyes. Her small face looked so comical peeping out from under the brim that Meg had to smile.

Folding the coat, Meg placed it in a box with other clothes to give away. Then, starting at the far end of the attic, she put trash in the empty cartons she'd brought with her and packed things to be kept in boxes which she then neatly tied with string. Finally, she straightened up and looked around. It was discouraging. She'd only made a dent in the accumulation of a lot of years. "Come on, Kathy," she said, wiping beads of perspiration off her forehead with the bottom of her T-shirt. "Let's go down and have some lunch. We'll finish this later."

After leaving his father at the boatyard, Lloyd walked through Honga to the swing bridge. There were traffic lights at each end, and black-and-white-striped gates to be lowered. The bridgetender sat in the shack that housed the machinery which activated the bridge. Lloyd leaned over the rail to watch the men fishing from rowboats nearby. Suddenly, three blasts of a horn made him look around. A power launch was coming from the Honga River headed for the Bay. The bridge started to swing. The bridgetender hadn't seen Lloyd. Lloyd ran the length of the bridge and jumped over the widening crack to the road beyond.

He trudged on. Even before the cleared, drained land that was destined to be a subdivision came into view, he heard the roar of the bulldozers. Around the bend the marsh lay spread out before him, destroyed to make room for people. People had to have homes, Lloyd knew. Still, it made him sad that this particular marsh had been taken— a marsh that had been used by song birds and waterfowl for nesting and feeding ever since birds were a part of creation.

Leaving the blacktop, he trudged across the cleared earth toward a bulldozer. The driver recognized him and stopped his machine. He was the same fellow Lloyd had talked to before.

"Hi, there, bud!" the man shouted. "Where've you been? I figured you'd be here near every day after school was out."

"We've had some other stuff goin'," Lloyd explained. "How're the geese?"

"Okay. We've stayed as far away as we could. I've been spreadin' a little corn around. Go take a look. You're goin' t'have a surprise!"

Lloyd hurried toward the tangle of bushes and tall grass that had been left standing to protect the geese. He pushed through the bushes, walking carefully. When he saw the heads of the geese, he dropped to his hands and knees, creeping forward until he had a good view of the nest. One of the birds was nestled down on it; the other, the gander, was watching nearby. Lloyd straightened his glasses. Then he caught his breath. There was a bit of yellow fluff near the goose's breast. As he watched, the gosling stepped onto the edge of the nest, stretched its little neck, and raised the tiny flaps that someday would be great, powerful wings. A grin spread over Lloyd's face, and he squirmed with pleasure. The geese turned their heads. Lloyd froze, and they went back to tending the nest.

He stayed there a long time watching. Another gosling appeared. He'd just chipped his way out of the egg, and his feathers were wet and stuck close to his body. Lloyd wanted desperately to see the other eggs hatch. He waited and waited. The sun beat down, making his shirt stick to his back, and the prickly grass under his stomach made his skin itch unmercifully.

Suddenly, gun shots: bang ... bang, bang! Lloyd looked up. A flock of ducks rose from the river. No birds fell, but he knew from experience that was only because some hunter had missed his aim. The goose lowered her head and gathered her goslings close. The gander took flight, flying unevenly toward the river to draw attention from his nest. Furious with the poacher who'd fired the shots, Lloyd backed out of the bushes determined to find him. This was the nesting season. All birds were protected by law. Mr. Prior had told Lloyd's class the day it visited Blackwater Wildlife Refuge that poaching should be reported. If he could find the culprit, Lloyd intended to do just that.

He ran across the cleared ground paralleling the river in the direction from which the shots had come. The ducks were circling high over the river now. Lloyd stumbled over big clods of loosened dirt, and his breath was coming in short gasps, but he kept on. He came to a tidal creek, wide and deep. To cross it he'd have to swim. He stood on its edge wondering what to do next when he saw the gander flying low near the shore on the other side. Lloyd longed to call out to him, *Go back! Go back, before it's too late!* As though in answer to his wish, the big bird banked into a slow upward turn, his powerfully stroking wings carrying him higher and higher. Lloyd held his breath. Then it happened. There was a shot. The gander's great wings crumpled, his head dropped, and he plummeted into the river with a splash. Immediately a dog swam out to retrieve him. The dog came from a duck blind on a point of land not fifty yards beyond the stream.

Filled with a painful mixture of rage and sorrow, Lloyd headed for the blacktop. A duck blind like that one was sure to be accessible from the road. If he knew who owned the land, that much at least could be reported to a game warden. When he reached the blacktop, he walked fast up a hill and around a bend. There he saw a driveway leading toward the river. On either side stood a fieldstone post. A chain was stretched between them. From the chain hung a sign—"Private Drive, No Trespassers."

Another sign nailed to a tree said, "Trespassers will be prosecuted to the full extent of the law." Frustrated, he looked around and saw a mailbox half-covered with ivy. He walked slowly over to it, pushed aside the vine, and read the name. It was Lester Messick.

Lloyd stood staring at the mailbox. It was hard to believe his uncle would permit shooting on his land out of season. Of course he might not know about it. On the other hand, Lloyd thought a little bitterly, he might be out there himself banging away! With hunched shoulders and dragging steps, he headed back down the blacktop toward Honga.

Driving home with his father late that afternoon, Lloyd tried to talk about it. "Dad, Uncle Lester has a place up on Meekins Neck, doesn't he?"

"Aye, along the Honga shore."

"When I was up there today, someone shot one of the pair of geese I've been watching, the gander."

Mr. Evans gave him a quick look, then turned again to the road. "I'm sorry to hear that, son. I know you set a lot of store by those geese."

"The shot came from a duck blind on a farm beyond that new subdivision. That his?"

"Could be. He has some blinds. Does well with them, too. Blinds in a good location like that sometimes rent for $5,000 a year."

"I saw the gander shot down, and a dog came from the duck blind after it. Shouldn't the warden be told, Dad?"

Mr. Evans rubbed his chin. "I'd not like makin' trouble for your Uncle Lester and Aunt Lavinia, Lloyd. You can't be certain the shootin' came from their place. You didn't see a man raise a gun."

"Maybe someone's trespassin', and Uncle Lester would like t'know about it. He might like t'know."

"I'd just as leave let it be."

Lloyd was disappointed in his father but said no more. He was torn between not wishing to go against his father's wishes and guilt at not reporting what he'd seen. And he was tired. By the time they reached home and he was telling Meg, all he felt was a dull sorrow, sorrow for the poor old goose left without a mate.

10

M EG WOKE EARLY the next morning and looked immediately out the window. The sky was overcast, but the curtains hung straight and still. She listened for sounds of her father stirring in his room across the hall. She didn't have to wait long. Jumping out of bed, she ran to his open door and saw him standing by the window.

"Is today the day, Dad?"

"Aye, it looks prime. No wind to speak of. We'll have a bite of breakfast, then drive to the boatyard."

By seven-thirty everyone was aboard the *J. P. Leonard*

and ready to start. Captain Noah gave the order to cast off the lines, and the big power boat pulled away from the dock.

As they chugged past the green sweep of lawn in front of the captain's house, Mrs. Whitelock waved from the veranda. She was a small round woman with a button nose and double chins. Her fluffy white hair was cut short. Her brown eyes, large and soft, were hidden behind thick-lensed spectacles, but her smile relayed encouragement to the group on the *Leonard*.

Meg sat on the forward deck with Jamie and Kathy beside her. They watched the bow wave curl like a white plume away from the *Leonard*'s hull. It was a still, gray morning; the surface of the Bay was as smooth as a dove's breast. Dead branches standing in the water to mark fishermen's nets looked like ghostly skeletons in the haze. Meg put her arm around Kathy. The air was damp and slightly chill, as the sun had not yet burned through. No one talked, not even Jamie. It was that kind of weather. The only sound was the steady chug of the *Leonard*'s engine.

All the equipment needed to salvage the *Tessie C. Price* was piled high in the cockpit—a gasoline engine, a pump, caulking compound, and plenty of lines. In the stern, Mr. Evans kept an eye on the twelve oil drums which he had lashed together into a raft and tied on behind.

Lloyd stood beside Captain Noah at the helm. The captain looked at his watch. "Ten to eight," he said. "High tide's at one thirty-five. By that time we should have the bugeye off the bottom of that creek and be ready t'move her out, make the most of high water."

"D'you think she'll come off okay?" Lloyd asked, his eyes anxious.

"It's hard t'tell till we give her a try."

They followed the channel between Hooper's Island and the mainland, sticking close to the buoys. A few fishermen had already anchored their rowboats near the swing bridge. Clamming boats were at work, their steel mesh scoops, attached to conveyor belts, scraping the bottom and bringing up anything that lay in their path. As the *Leonard* approached the bridge, Captain Noah gave the customary three blasts on his horn, a signal for the bridgetender to open up. The man was in no hurry. Captain Noah shifted into neutral gear so as not to ram the bridge. Meanwhile the young Evanses waited impatiently for something to happen. Finally, the bridgetender changed the traffic lights to red and lowered the gates. After a car or two had stopped, he activated the machinery that turned the bridge. The gears grated; the bridge creaked and slowly disengaged itself from the roadways. Captain Noah put his engine in forward gear and eased the *J. P. Leonard* through.

They headed south on the Honga River along the shore of upper Hooper's. Though most of the river was shallow, the dredged channel had water enough and to spare for the *Leonard*, which drew only three and a half feet. But the channel was narrow. The captain took care to take the buoys correctly, red nuns to port, black cans to starboard. They passed close to a tall pole that held a beacon for boats coming in after dark. On top of it a pair of osprey had built their nest, an untidy affair of interwoven sticks and marsh grass. The male stood on its edge, but the female was nestled down with only her head showing. Meg took out her drawing pad and quickly sketched in their outlines.

They came to the end of upper Hooper's and crossed the small-boat channel that led to the Bay. The children could see the causeway and plank bridge near their house, then the piney woods. Far down the Honga the great hulk of a wrecked freighter was canted at a crazy angle against the sky. It had been there for years.

"The creek where the bugeye lies is just 'round that point," Captain Noah said. "We'll soon have t'leave the channel and work our way up it. If we're not careful, the bottom will grab us sure! Lloyd, get out the lead line and be ready t'sound."

He steered the boat around the point, then slowed to a couple of knots.

"I see the *Tessie*'s masts!" Meg shouted, jumping up. "See them sticking up out of the marsh?"

Mr. Evans had a pair of binoculars. "That's her all right! Bear to the starboard, Noah. I see the creek's mouth."

Captain Noah turned the wheel to the right, and they left the dredged channel. "Begin soundin', Lloyd," he said.

Lloyd threw the lead into the water and checked the yellow plastic markers on the line. "Four feet and a half!" he called.

"So far, so good," the captain said. "That leaves us a foot of water under our bottom. It's goin' t'be tight as we get in close. Keep soundin', Lloyd."

The *J. P. Leonard* moved slowly forward.

"Four feet, two inches!" Lloyd called. He kept on checking the lead line every few minutes. The water held at around four feet. They entered the mouth of the creek. Lloyd threw the lead. "Three feet and—no inches!" Lloyd's voice squeaked with dismay.

The next instant the *Leonard* hit bottom, bumping three or four times like a car on a rutted road, then stopping altogether. The raft of oil drums came up on the stern and banged into the transom. Captain Noah threw the engine into reverse. But it was too late. The *Leonard* was hard aground.

"What'll we do now, Cap'n Noah?" Meg asked, wringing her hands. The *Tessie* had seemed so close! Now perhaps they'd never reach her.

"The mud's not been invented that'll hold the *Leonard*," he replied. "It may take a few minutes, but we'll work our way free." He switched off the engine and circled the deck, poking his boathook into the mud to determine where the greatest depth lay. Several times he asked Lloyd to drop the lead. Then, settling himself again in the helmsman's seat, he eased the engine into reverse, gradually increased the rpm's, and turned the wheel hard over to the port side.

The propeller churned up mud from the bottom and the oil drums bobbled uncertainly, but the boat didn't move. To the young Evanses it seemed an untimely end to a great expedition. They sat on the deck, their eyes fixed longingly on the masts of the *Tessie C. Price*. It had been pleasantly cool while the boat was moving. Now that they were motionless, there was no breeze and the sun beat down hotter and hotter. The engine roared in their ears, and the smell of burning oil was almost sickening.

"It's just a matter of time," Captain Noah said, seeing their discouraged faces. "The stream of water that prop shoots at the bottom will dig us outta the mud. Has lots of times before. If we was hung up on rock, it'd be different! That's one good thing 'bout Chesapeake country. Though it's shallow lots of places, the bottom's mostly mud. The tide's comin' in, too. That'll help."

Suddenly, the *Leonard* lurched backward, knocking the oil drums together with a clang. The hull humped over a high place, and all at once they were free.

"Yippee!" Jamie shouted. "We're off!"

Meg sighed with relief.

The captain altered course slightly, and the *Leonard* continued up the creek. Bottom grazed bottom several times, but the boat kept moving ahead. They came around a bend, and there she was in full view, the *Tessie C. Price*.

"Look at her!" Jamie shouted, defying balance as he hung over the rail in the *Leonard*'s bow. "She's bigger'n I remembered!"

"And prettier, too!" Lloyd exclaimed.

Meg just looked and looked. Her eyes couldn't get enough of the *Tessie*.

Captain Noah edged the *Leonard* up under her bow. Grabbing her bowsprit, Mr. Evans swung onto the *Tessie*'s deck and made the *Leonard* fast. The boys scrambled aboard, and Meg swung Kathy over to her father. Then she, too, climbed aboard.

Then the task of floating the *Tessie C. Price* began.

"Give me a hand with this pump, Tyler," the captain said. "There's no time to lose! We've only a couple of hours till high tide!"

The men set up the pump on the *Tessie*'s deck and put it to work emptying her hull. To hasten its work, the Evans family bailed by hand as well. Mr. Evans stood in the companionway, waist deep in water, filled a bucket, and passed it to Lloyd—who passed it to Meg, who passed it to Jamie at the rail, who dumped it over the side. Kathy trotted back with the empty bucket. Meanwhile another full bucket was on its way. Captain Noah kept an eye on the pump to be sure it was operating efficiently.

107

After the level of the water had gone down several feet, Mr. Evans began caulking leaks as they became evident. Lloyd took his place in the companionway. Before long the hull was almost dry.

"Time out for lunch!" Captain Noah said. "She's wantin' t'float. After we've eaten, we'll see if the *Leonard* can give her the encouragement she needs."

Meg handed out sandwiches. They ate hurriedly, washing their food down with orange soda. The tide was almost at the flood.

"Jeepers, it's hot!" Jamie said, taking a final gulp of soda. "Wanta see a neat trick?" Without waiting for an answer he sat on the rail, brought his knees up to his chin, and somersaulted backward into the water.

Kathy was slumped against the doghouse.

"Lollipop, you look like a wilted pink petunia," Meg said. "It's time you had a nap." With help from her father, Meg got Kathy over onto the *Leonard*. In its cabin Kathy curled up on a bunk, and Meg covered her with an old jacket of the captain's.

When she rejoined the others, Captain Noah said, "All right now, if everybody's ready, let's move 'er out. Tyler, free the oil drums." To Jamie, who was still in the water, he said, "You can push the oil drums into place around her hull and hold them while your father and I make 'em fast. Lloyd, you'd better help him."

Lloyd took off his glasses and jumped into the creek. He and Jamie swam and waded after oil drums as they were released, herding them back toward the *Tessie*. The men were ready with lots of line. With the boys' help they lashed the oil drums into place, passing lines under the *Tessie*'s keel where there was clearance. Wherever they could, they pulled the drums under water to give extra buoyancy.

"Now I'm goin' to turn the *Leonard*," Captain Noah said, climbing aboard the power boat. "Cast me off!"

The big power boat chugged forward and back until it was headed downstream and had its stern under the bugeye's bowsprit. Next the men attached a towing line. Captain Noah settled himself firmly in the helmsman's seat and started his engine. He eased it slowly into forward gear. Everyone held his breath, eyes on the line between the boats as it grew taut. The captain gradually increased the rpm's. There was a painful creaking of timbers, but the *Tessie* didn't budge. Would she fall apart plank by plank before the bottom let her go? Meg wondered.

Captain Noah left the helm of the *Leonard* and walked back. He tested the depth of the water under the *Tessie*'s bow with his boat hook. "There's enough water here," he said. "It's her keel aft that's down in the mud. The lot of you stand on her bowsprit. When I say jump, jump! Mebbe your weight will jostle her loose."

All the Evanses stood on the bowsprit, holding onto the stays and each other. The captain revved his engine. "Jump!" he shouted.

They bounced up and down until they were breathless and dripping with perspiration. It was no use. The *Tessie* hadn't moved.

The captain came back once more. "All right. We'll try somethin' else. Into the water with you. Try and push her sideways off that mud into midstream. I'll give you all the help I can."

Meg slid into the water after her father and brothers.

They stood waist deep on the shallow side of the *Tessie's* stern, palms flat against her hull. Captain Noah lengthened the towing line between the boats and moved the *Leonard* out into midstream so he'd be pulling at an angle rather than dead ahead. "All right. Shove!" he yelled, revving his engine.

The Evanses shoved with all their might. Meg felt her feet sink deeper and deeper into the mud. Suddenly, she was bending forward. "She's moving!" she gasped.

"Praise be!" her father said. "She's on her way."

Meg's tired muscles were trembling, but excitement kept her going. They kept on shoving. Another minute, and the *Tessie C. Price* moved out of her muddy grave and was floating free.

A shout of triumph from the young Evanses startled a muskrat, who looked up from the root he was gnawing and slipped into the creek. The great blue heron stretched his neck to see what was going on, then went back to hunting frogs among the reeds.

Mrs. Whitelock had put off weeding her flower border until the sun lost some of its heat. Now, with trowel and kneeling pad in hand, she ventured out of the coolness of her high-ceilinged living room. She placed the pad on the grass and knelt on it, wincing with a twinge of arthritis as she did so. Feeling among the zinnias and petunias for weed stems, she pulled out one after another. Yanking out a thick, prickly thistle she said, "There! That'll be the end of you. And good riddance, too! You're bullies, the lot of you, pushin' in where you're not wanted, hardly leavin' room for my posies t'breathe!" With her trowel she dug deep to get the whole of a tough dandelion root.

Holding up the offending plant, she looked at it triumphantly. "And now I have *you*, sir, and I'll thank you to keep your seeds out of my garden in the future!"

She moved slowly down the border, scolding the weeds and sweet-talking the flowers. At last she reached the end and stood up, carefully straightening her back. "You're a pretty lot," she said to her flowers, "but you want a heap o' lookin' after!"

Turning from her flower border, she looked out across Tar Bay toward the channel. The folks should be coming back before long, she thought, dragging that old boat—that is, if they've managed to get her off in one piece. She wondered how it would be having a family of lively children living by her picket fence. She wasn't used to the noise and confusion of a young family any more. Her own children had long since married and moved away. They visited every summer, of course. In fact, her grandson Peter would be coming down next week to do some sailing. Peter might enjoy the Evanses' company; she would just have to see.

She walked down the sloping lawn and stood at the edge of the water, shading her eyes against the sun. She saw a sailboat far out beyond Barren Island, its white wings spread to catch the light airs, and some fishing boats heading in, but no sign of Noah's *Leonard*.

She put her gardening things away, then went into the kitchen to take a peek at the pot roast she had in the oven. It smelled real good! She had always said that a few slices of onion and a pinch of herbs did wonders for a piece of meat. She wondered how Meg Evans was managing. It was a lot of responsibility she had, and Tyler, though a pious man and a skilled worker, was not one to lean on in practical matters. She'd heard there was an aunt who wanted to take the baby. Personally she liked to see families stick together through thick and thin.

Closing the oven door, she walked out onto the veranda to look again for Noah. It was the time of day she liked best. The air had begun to cool, and the light was golden on the trees and water. She went down the steps and stood by the white oak. The oak had already been a fine tree when the house was built forty years ago. Now it had doubled its size. Old Skipper came to join her.

The sun hung in the clear sky, a huge red glowing ball just above the horizon. Not a wisp of cloud marred its roundness. All at once she heard the chug of an engine. The sound was faint but rapidly grew louder. Then she saw the *Leonard* coming around the bend pulling the old bugeye. Her hull looked misshapen because of the oil drums lashed along her sides. The *Leonard* passed in front of the sun, followed a few seconds later by the bugeye, her silhouette tall against the sun's red face. Her bowsprit touched its edge like a pointed finger, and her raked masts were slanting black bars.

11

THE NEXT DAY Captain Noah arranged to have a heavy-duty tractor come to the boatyard and beach the *Tessie C. Price*. The men dug a shallow trench to hold her keel so that her decks would be level. Then she was hauled in and positioned with her stern to the boatyard and her bowsprit sticking out over the water.

After work Mr. Evans brought his family back to look at her. The captain sauntered over to join them. Seeing the *Tessie* beached, even Meg felt momentarily discouraged. The ship's bottom was crusted with scabby brown barnacles, while furry green algae fringed her sides.

Mrs. Whitelock came through the gate in her picket fence to see what was going on. She took one look at the *Tessie*, then marched over to the captain. "Noah, she's awful close to our fence and no more'n a whoop and a holler from our veranda!"

"This is the best place for her, Bessie," the captain replied. "The land lies low here, so we were able to slide her up easy. She's downhill from the store. That'll let water flow into her galley at a good rate."

"She's hardly a thing of beauty—I'll say that—with her paint peelin' off and that rail broke. Her bottom looks rotten as a bad apple!"

Meg overheard. "We'll clean her up, Mrs. Whitelock," she said, rising to the *Tessie*'s defense. "When she's painted and repaired she'll look grand! You'll see."

"Well, I hope you're right, young lady!"

In spite of Mrs. Whitelock's tartness, Kathy had taken a fancy to her. She liked her comfortable roundness, her fluffy white hair and pink cheeks.

"We've a kitty cat." Kathy beamed up into her face. "Her name's Scaredy."

"Scaredy? Is she scared of somethin'?" Mrs. Whitelock looked mildly surprised.

"Yes'm." Kathy nodded her head. "Most everything."

Jamie swung up onto the *Tessie*'s bowsprit and climbed out to the end. "Hey! It's far enough out to jump into the water. That'll be neat for swimmin'!"

Lloyd stood quietly at the edge of the water, letting his eyes travel over the old ship from bowsprit to transom and back again. He thought of finding her just a week ago out in the marsh, a million miles from nowhere. To think she was beached now, ready for them to go to work on! It fairly made him dizzy.

Meg stood quietly, too. But she wasn't seeing the *Tessie* at all. She was thinking about Mrs. Whitelock. Was it going to be uncomfortable living next door to the old lady? She wished she were as easygoing as the captain. The boys would have to keep a lid on their noise, and the Whitelock house and yard had better be out of bounds.

The days remaining before moving day, the third of July, marched steadily on. Mr. Evans worked on the *Tessie* every moment he could spare from his regular job, making the most of the long June days. He put a partition across the cabin with a door in it. In the forward section he built bunks on either side for the girls. The boys would sleep in the fo'c'sle. A bunk in the main cabin aft would be his, doubling as a sitting place. The dining table hung on hinges flat against a bulkhead and could be lowered when needed. The galley stretched across the stern. Eventually he would panel the entire interior, but right now he concentrated on making the *Tessie* livable.

The boys helped, scraping and painting the hull. Even Jamie showed real dedication. One afternoon they were putting a second coat of paint on her deck, taking care not to paint themselves away from the boarding ladder their father had nailed to her side. It was a sunny afternoon with a brisk breeze that set the branches on the trees in the Whitelocks' yard to dancing and sailboats to scudding along out on the Bay. Jamie's eyes traveled up the mainmast.

"Lloyd, what she needs is a flag! A good ship always flies a flag."

"New flags are expensive," Lloyd said, wiping a spot of paint off his nose. "We could ask Dad."

Meg wielded a paintbrush when she could and took on the considerable job of making covers for the bunk cushions out of some faded blue curtains. Cutting and sewing the material to precise measurements was more tiresome than she ever could have imagined. Those for the fo'c'sle had to be a strange pointy shape to fit the bow. She was making slow progress.

A few days before moving day, Mr. Evans borrowed the pickup truck from the boatyard, loaded it with worn-out furniture, and took it to a second-hand dealer in Cambridge. They hoped it would bring enough to pay for the foam rubber for the bunks, an ice chest, and a stainless steel sink. Captain Noah had offered to lend them an alcohol stove.

"Sink had t'be ordered," Mr. Evans told Meg when he returned. "They didn't have the right size in stock. Think we can manage with a basin for washin' up time bein'?"

"Sure," she said, confident she could manage most anything on the *Tessie*.

On moving day the pickup truck traveled back and forth from the house to the boatyard all morning. Meg did the organizing. "Lloyd, that's no way to pack dishes. Each one has to be wrapped separately, or— Jamie, where d'you think you're goin' with those stacks of comic books? Now, you just turn around and head for the trash."

"But Meg, it's my collection! All my favorites—"

"Carry them out back. There'll be no room for that sort of thing on the *Tessie*. And Lloyd, you'll have to leave the stuffed owl. It has moths."

"Oh gee, Meg, I thought it'd look good stuck up in the peak of the fo'c'sle."

When Jamie came back, Meg was ready for him. "Now, go up and bring down all the clothes in my closet. Lloyd will help you."

"Jeepers creepers, Meg! I'm tired of you givin' orders

around here! You're a big pain!" He sat down on the floor cross-legged. "I'm not movin' from this spot till I'm good and ready."

Lloyd grinned. "You are being kinda bossy, Meg. Why don't you relax? We'll get it done."

Meg pushed her damp hair off her perspiring forehead and slumped down in the one remaining chair. "Okay, fellas. Sorry." She thought a moment. "Let's say you can take anything you can fit in the fo'c'sle, but no more."

"Fair enough," Lloyd agreed, picking up his owl.

Jamie went out back to rescue a few choice comic books.

The truck came for its last load, and the boys went back to the boatyard with it to help with the unloading at the other end. Kathy was on the back porch playing with her kitten.

The empty house looked strangely quiet and forlorn. All its defects showed plainly now that the furnishings were gone. There were places where the paint was peeling, places where the floor boards were soft. Meg saw a broom standing in the corner of the hall and began sweeping. She didn't like to leave her mother's house with dirt on the floor.

She swept kitchen, living room, and hall, taking a long look at the steep stairs that had so changed their lives. She shivered. At that moment the truck drove up. Meg went out the back door aware that she was closing it for the last time. She scooped up Scaredy, took Kathy by the hand, and walked around the house to the truck without looking back.

Mr. Evans parked the truck at the end of the boathouse. The boys were already at work storing their excess furniture in the loft. Meg and Kathy headed for the *Tessie* to

117

introduce Scaredy to her new home. Kathy insisted on carrying the kitten herself. Suddenly, Scaredy caught sight of Old Skipper, jumped out of Kathy's arms, and ran off. Kathy squealed in dismay.

"Don't worry, lollipop," Meg said. "She'll find us when she gets hungry."

Meg took sandwiches to her father and the boys, then found a corner in the fo'c'sle where Kathy could nap. Family belongings covered the bunks and cluttered the floor. She stowed things as best she could and washed the portholes, polishing them until they shone like a fussy old lady's spectacles. After she'd finished, she stood back to admire her work. The world looked different through a porthole. It became a small blue saucer, displaying only a wisp of cloud and a newly leaved branch.

Hearing heavy footsteps on the deck, she glanced toward the companionway. Boots appeared on the steps, legs, then the captain's stout body. He was carrying the alcohol stove he'd promised. "Say, you're makin' real progress!" he said, stepping down into the cabin.

Meg glowed with pleasure.

He fitted the stove into the place on the galley counter Mr. Evans had prepared for it, then hung a small red fire extinguisher on the cabin wall beside it. "Alcohol can be tricky stuff," he explained. "If you let too much run into the pan before you light it, it flames up somethin' fierce! It's good to have this thing handy just in case."

"I'll be careful, Cap'n Noah. Thank you."

"Don't mention it, honey. We're glad t'have you nearby, me and Mis' Whitelock."

"Is she really? I hope we won't bother her or be in her way, or anything."

The captain chuckled. "Her bark's considerably

worse'n her bite, I can tell you that. Fact is, she asked me to invite you all over for supper. She says nobody ought to have to cook on movin' day!"

"That's nice, Cap'n Noah. Tell her thanks; we'd like that."

"Righto. We'll expect you 'round six. Come topsides with me, Meg. Somethin' I'd like you t'see."

Meg followed the captain up the companionway. Looking beyond Barren Island to the Bay, she saw a fleet of large sailboats bearing down on Hooper's Island.

"The skipjacks!" Captain Noah said. "Comin' in for the race tomorrow."

Meg watched with admiration as the sails rose and dipped in a stately dance ordered by the motion of the water. "And your *Nellie Byrd* is goin' to take them all?" She cast a sidelong glance at the captain.

"You bet, honey! Your dad and I took her out on a trial run day afore yesterday, and she stepped out real lively. I asked your brother Lloyd if he'd like t'come along tomorrow and crew. He seems willin'."

Meg bit her lip. She would have liked to be asked.

Soon after Captain Noah left, Kathy woke up. "Scaredy back?"

"No, lollipop. We'll ask the boys. Maybe they've seen her."

Together they walked over to the boathouse. All the things that had been standing about were now stowed aloft. Mr. Evans stood in the rear of the truck holding the last box high. Jamie reached for it, lost his balance, and fell forward. He caught the bottom edge of the door frame with one hand and hung suspended, his feet kicking air. Meg screamed. Mr. Evans dropped the box and reached for Jamie's legs. Jamie's hand slipped. With a yell, he landed on top of his father. Mr. Evans staggered backward, and they ended in a heap on the floor of the truck.

"Jamie! Dad!" Meg exclaimed, running toward them. "Are you hurt?"

Lloyd slid down the ladder and pulled Jamie off his father. Mr. Evans sat up, rubbing his elbow.

"No bones broke, I reckon. You all right, Jamie?"

"My hand hurts!" he cried. "Look! It's bleeding!"

There was a large splinter in the palm of his hand and a bloody gouge across it.

"Why can't you be more careful, Jamie Evans?" Meg scolded. "You scared the livin' daylights outta me!"

Tears were making channels in the dirt on Jamie's face. "I didn't fall on purpose!" he blubbered. "D'you think I fell on purpose, you dumb old girl?"

"Take it easy, you two," their father said. "Meg, no use scolding. Accidents will happen. Jamie, you can stop crying now. I don't doubt you'll survive." He slid from the truck and helped Jamie down. "Go wash your hands and face. Then I'll take the splinter out. We're all tired . . ."

"Come along, Jamie," Meg said, putting her arm around his shoulder. She felt sorry she'd been cross. She knew she should have more patience. After all, Jamie was a lot younger than she and Lloyd.

That evening at supper there was considerable talk about the next day's events.

"On the Fourth of July," Jamie said, his mouth full of mashed potatoes, "a ship should fly a flag! The *Tessie* needs a flag."

"A flag," Mrs. Whitelock mused. "I b'lieve there's an old flag in our attic we've no use for. It only has forty-eight stars, but folks would hardly notice that. By the way, did I mention that Sarah's comin' down with her family tomorrow? Tom, that's our son-in-law, and Peter are goin' t'crew for the captain in the skipjack race."

By the time supper was over, the Evanses were ready to call it a day. Jamie went to the attic with the captain to find the old flag. Then the Evanses bid the Whitelocks goodnight and headed for the *Tessie*. Meg and Lloyd made up the bunks while the younger children got into their pajamas. Jamie stowed the old flag under his bunk cushion for safekeeping.

"In the morning I'll find some white cloth and make two more stars," Meg promised. "I can sew them onto the blue."

"Thanks, Meg," Jamie said. "You're okay."

Meg gave him a hug. "You are too, Jamie."

Meg found her bunk harder and smaller than the bed she'd had in the old house. But she rather liked its smallness. It was snug. It was a good feeling to know that Kathy was there just across the cabin, her father settled in the main cabin, and the boys in the fo'c'sle. She had faith in the *Tessie*, faith that she'd help keep the family together, holding them close in her gently curving timbers.

12

I T WAS TYPICAL Fourth of July weather, hot and
still. The skipjacks hung on their anchors near the
shore. The more hopeful captains had raised their
sails, but they hung limp as old rags, their reflections
making wavery white triangles on the water.

Jamie lay across the bunk in the *Tessie*'s main cabin on
his stomach, his sneakers resting against a porthole and
his head hanging over the edge. He was lazily turning the
pages of a comic book. Kathy sat in the corner mourning
the loss of her kitten. "I've looked 'n looked 'n looked,"
she said sadly. "No Scaredy! Not any place!"

Meg put down the white cloth she was cutting into

stars. "We'll find her, Kathy. I'm sure of it. Jamie, take Kathy and look around the boatyard one more time. Maybe the stupid little thing climbed up into the boathouse loft and got shut in."

"Not stupid thing!" Kathy objected.

"Okay, lollipop. Whatever you say. Please, Jamie. I want to finish the flag."

Reluctantly Jamie closed his comic book and started up the companionway with Kathy at his heels.

Meg succeeded in getting two star shapes out of the cloth. She decided to sew one in the top left corner of the blue and the other in the bottom right. She was just finishing the last point when she heard a boy's voice calling, "Hello! Hello aboard the *Tessie C. Price!*"

Fastening her thread, she broke it and dropped the needle into her sewing box. Then she tucked in her shirttail, brushed some stray wisps of hair back off her face, and climbed up on deck. A tall, slim teen-ager stood at the bottom of the boarding ladder. He had a freckled face, friendly brown eyes, and a lopsided grin. She found his wavy, reddish-brown hair attractive.

"Hi!" he said. "Permission to come aboard?"

She smiled. "Come ahead. You Peter?"

The boy nodded and started up the ladder. "The others are in the house with Grandma. But I couldn't wait to see your ship and who lives on her."

"Well, I'm one. Then there's Kathy and Jamie. Lloyd and Dad have gone out to the *Nellie Byrd* with your grandfather. Lloyd's going t'crew."

Peter walked to the bow and looked over the water toward the skipjacks. "It's rotten luck, this calm weather! I hope they don't call the race."

"Your grandfather's going t'be awful disappointed if

they do! He's been talking about how he was going to beat his pal, Jake Parks, for days!"

Meg climbed out to the end of the bowsprit. Peter followed and they stood there holding onto the stays, watching the skipjacks. Their sails still hung motionless.

"Has your brother ever crewed before?"

"Not in a race. He's really excited. We don't get a lot of chances to go sailing, but I think it's the most fun in all the world!"

"Why aren't you going along today?"

"I wasn't invited."

"Why not?"

"Well, you see there's Kathy. I couldn't ..."

"Maybe someone else could keep an eye on Kathy. I'll go ask my grandfather to let you go—that is, if there's a race." Peter started for the boarding ladder, but Meg grabbed his arm.

"Don't do that, please."

"Why not? You want to go, don't you?" His brown eyes studied her quizzically.

"Yes, but crewin's something special. You don't go 'round getting yourself asked. Besides, I expect Lloyd will have a better time without me. Who needs a big sister around at a time like that? I'm not explaining it very well."

"Sure you are."

Meg suddenly realized she still had her hand on his arm and took it away embarrassed. "Then you won't say anything to your grandfather?"

"No, if you'd rather I didn't. But d'you know what I think? I think your brother's lucky to have you for a sister. And the next time I go sailing around here, *you're* going with me, not Lloyd."

Meg felt her face grow warm. "I'd like that."

"Count on it." His face broke into a wide grin.

"Come on. I'll show you the rest of the boat."

They climbed down the companionway, and Peter saw the flag. "What're you going t'do with that?"

"Get it to the top of the mast, if it's any way possible. It's a funny flag. Your grandmother gave it to us. I had to sew on two more stars."

"It's not bad—better than leaving out Alaska and Hawaii altogether."

"That's what I thought."

"Is there some line about? Something we could use for a halyard?"

"There's lots of line in the boathouse."

Together they went for the line. Peter also picked up a small pulley, a hammer, and some nails. Back on the *Tessie*, Peter tied one end of the line to his belt, put the other things in his pocket, and shinnied up the mast.

"Hey," he called down. "The old shive's still here. That'll make it easy!" Clinging to the mast with one arm, his long legs wrapped around the mast, he passed the line through the shive and slid down. Then he tied the ends of the line securely into the eyelets of the flag and began hoisting.

Meg watched expectantly as the flag traveled up the mast. But when it reached the top, it hung lifeless, a sagging bit of red, white, and blue cloth. Meg said, disappointment plain in her face, "It doesn't look like much without a breeze, does it? A flag needs a breeze."

Peter stared at it thoughtfully. "Have you heard about a knife in the mast to bring wind?"

She shook her head. Peter took a fishing knife from his pocket and threw it with a flip of his wrist. The point buried itself in the mast, and the knife hung there quivering. Again they looked to the top of the mast. Nothing had changed. Meg turned to look at the skipjacks. All was as before. She looked questioningly at Peter, and he shrugged his shoulders.

"Never hurts to try," he said. "Guess I'll go find out what's been decided about the race. Sure you won't change your mind?"

"Yeah. Good luck."

"See you later."

He had reached the top of the ladder when Meg felt a tiny breath of air on her cheek. Looking up she saw a corner of the flag twitch. She blinked her eyes and looked again. The flag was fluttering ever so slightly. "Peter!" she called. "Look at that flag! I just don't believe it!"

Peter stood with his head thrown back, his hands on his hips, looking at the flag, and his eyes sparkled. "What did I tell you? It's an old seaman's trick."

As they watched, the flag unfurled itself and stood out straight and stiff from the mast.

Meg burst out laughing. "It worked, Peter! It worked!"

"First time it ever has that I know of." Peter was grinning all over his face. He started down the ladder taking the rungs two at a time. "I'd better get Dad. Looks like there's going t'be a race after all!"

Tingling with excitement, Meg climbed out onto the bowsprit again to watch the start of the race. From her vantage point she could see that the sails had come to life and were slatting restlessly from side to side. Men and boys scurried about making things fast and getting ready to weigh anchor. Dinghies were sent ashore or hoisted into davits, and the Committee Boat positioned itself at the starting line.

"Has it started?" Excitement made Jamie's voice shrill as he and Kathy ran across the boatyard, scrambled up the ladder and across the *Tessie*'s deck toward Meg.

"No. But you'd better hurry if you want to see it."

They sat as far out on the bowsprit as they could, their feet dangling over the water, and watched their father rowing the Dawsons out to the *Nellie Byrd*. Peter waved at Meg and she waved back.

"He your boyfriend, Meg?" Jamie asked slyly.

"Shut up, you little creep!"

"Meg's got a boyfriend! Meg's got a—"

Before he could finish, Meg gave a quick shove and he landed in the water. Kathy's eyes flew open wide. Jamie sputtered and splashed around in the water beneath them, and Meg rocked back and forth with laughter. Seeing her merriment, Kathy giggled. "Silly Jamie! All wet!"

Jamie shook his fist at his sisters in mock rage. "Just you wait, Meg Evans!"

At that moment the girls heard a bang and saw a puff of white smoke blossoming above the Committee Boat.

"Firecracker?" Kathy grabbed Meg.

"No, lollipop. That's the five-minute gun. Now sit still."

Jamie appeared on deck once more. Though he was dripping wet, he had regained his swagger. "Y'know, Meg, that felt super! Thanks a lot. Weather hot as this, you can do that any time you like."

"Well, I'm glad I have your permission. It may come in handy."

The skipjacks began jockeying for position, all hoping to be first over the line. Mr. Evans was rowing back to the dock. He was going to mind the boatyard during the race. The wind took the *Nellie Byrd*'s sails, and she was

127

almost to the starting line with several minutes yet to go. Peter sat at the helm, his chin lifted and his hair blowing in the wind. All at once Captain Noah grabbed the wheel. The *Nellie Byrd*'s sails began to shudder.

"Why'd he do that?" Jamie asked.

"To put her bow into the wind and stall her. He doesn't want to cross the starting line before the final gun."

Overanxious, the *Rosie Parks*, Jake Parks' skipjack, had done just that. Jake had to bring her about, turn back, and come up again. The *Amy Mister* was to windward of the *Nellie Byrd* and coming up fast. The *Peregrine North* lagged cautiously behind, as did the *John W. Kelso*.

Meg could see Peter's father standing near Captain Noah. He was looking at his wrist. She could imagine he was calling off the seconds marked by his watch, fifty-five, fifty, forty-five...

The starting gun went off. Captain Noah let the *Nellie Byrd*'s bow fall off the wind. The main sail flattened and she heeled over on a starboard tack. Her bowsprit crossed the line a split second later. A cheer went up from her deck. The *Nellie Byrd* had made a perfect start.

Late that afternoon the skipjacks came into sight again, stretched in a straight line across the Bay. The wind had gone down, and they seemed to hang motionless on the horizon. The glare of midday was softening into gold as the sun dropped lower in the sky.

Mrs. Whitelock and Peter's mother stood on the end of the main dock to watch the finish of the race. The young Evanses walked over to join them. Then their father came out. The skipjacks were still too far away for anyone to make a guess as to the outcome. The watchers on the dock waited patiently for positions to become clear.

At length Mr. Evans said, " 'Pears t'me the *Rosie Parks* is ahead. Old Jake must've done some fancy sailin' t'make up for his lame start. He has himself quite a lead. The next two, one could be the *Nellie Byrd*, either her or the *Amy Mister*. Can't tell for sure."

Meg's heart sank. She had so wanted the *Nellie Byrd* to win, not only for Captain Noah's sake, but for Lloyd's and Peter's too.

The skipjacks were slowly getting closer. The *Rosie Parks* was in the lead, followed by the *Nellie Byrd*. Next came the *Amy Mister*. The others were far behind. Before long it began to look to Meg as though the *Nellie Byrd* was narrowing the gap between her and the *Rosie Parks*. Jamie climbed onto a piling to see better and began waving his arms and shouting. "Come on, *Nellie Byrd!*"

"Daddy, me see too," Kathy said.

Mr. Evans hoisted her onto his shoulder. "Seems like they've all of a sudden learned how t'sail on the *Nellie Byrd*," he said. "Or they could've caught a favorable gust. She's comin' up good, now."

"D'you think she can close the gap, Dad?" Meg asked. Her heart was beating fast with excitement. "Do you?"

"The way she's picked up, if the race lasts long enough—"

"Come on, *Nellie Byrd!*" Jamie shouted again.

Close to the Barren Island light, the *Nellie Byrd* slipped past the *Rosie Parks* to leeward. They were in the lead at last. As they approached the finish line, the *Nellie Byrd* held half a boat's length on the *Rosie Parks*. But the *Rosie Parks* had the better position. There was an unexpected puff of wind. It reached the *Rosie Parks* first. She moved ahead fast. There was a puff of smoke, a bang, and the race was over. The *Rosie Parks* had won by a bowsprit. A few seconds later the *Nellie Byrd* crossed the line, rating a second gun. The other skipjacks were far behind.

That evening the Whitelocks, Dawsons, and Evanses found places on the deck of the *Tessie C. Price*, a vantage point from which to watch the Honga fireworks display over the water. There were folding chairs for the ladies. The young people settled themselves on the deck. Mr. Evans leaned against the mast talking to Captain Noah. " 'Fore you race again, I aim to alter the *Nellie*'s riggin'. There must be some way to flatten her sail, make it more taut so's she'll point better. Now, Jake Parks's sail . . ."

"That scoundrel!" Captain Noah growled good-naturedly. "Sneakin' up and takin' my wind! Next time it'll be different. Every boat has peculiarities. First time racin' you don't know her strengths and weaknesses."

"Second place is no disgrace," Tom Dawson said.

"Well, I had a right smart crew! No complaints about that!"

"Cap'n Noah, sing about Barnacle Bill!" Kathy looked up pleadingly from her place on the deck by the captain's feet.

Captain Noah couldn't resist an audience. He cleared his throat and sang in a deep bass, "It's only me from over the sea . . ." When he came to the part of the fair young maiden, his voice changed magically to a falsetto. He finished with a bellow that had Kathy clutching his leg in mock fright.

The afterglow had gone from the sky, leaving it purplish black and velvety. Meg and Peter crawled out to the end of the bowsprit, where they sat close together.

"I hated for you not to win the race. It was so close!"

"Well, it was a rip-roaring good sail anyway. On the way out, we were taking waves over the bow and heeling so the sails almost touched the water. You would have loved it!"

"I'm sure of that. Remember, you said we're going sailing together one day."

"Don't worry. I'm not likely to forget."

"What are you going to do the rest of the summer?"

"I had thought of hitch-hiking up to New England. Maine, maybe. I might get a job on one of those down-east schooners. Some of them are in the charter business."

"Oh."

There was a whooshing sound, and the first rocket of the evening streaked skyward, leaving a golden path of glowing embers behind it. Halfway up the sky it burst into a pompon of green spangles, its image mirrored in the still, dark water below. They watched burst after multicolored burst in silence. Meg hardly noticed when Peter took her hand.

The display was almost over when they heard the crunch of gravel in the driveway. Headlights probed the darkness. Car doors slammed, and a woman's voice called, "That you, Tyler?"

Meg's insides contracted into a hard knot. The voice was Aunt Lavinia's.

"Oh, rats." Meg sighed as other voices broke the stillness.

"What's the matter?" Peter helped her to her feet. "Who's that?"

"My aunt."

"She sounds upset about something."

"She's always upset about something."

They walked slowly aft. Captain Noah was leaning over the rail. "Ahoy there, Mrs. Messick! Can I give you a hand? We're watchin' the fireworks."

"No, thank you, Cap'n. I have no intention of climbin' that ladder. We hadn't heard from Tyler for a couple of weeks, so we drove down t'see what had become of him and the kids. It's taken us half the evening just to find them." The hostility in her voice was obvious. "And I must say—"

The whoosh of another rocket drowned her words. As a shower of gold trickled gently down the sky, Mrs. Whitelock struggled out of her deck chair. "We'll be goin' along, Tyler, now you've got company."

"Likely you've the right idea at that, Bessie," Captain Noah said. "Come on, kids! Let's clear out so the Evanses can visit with their relations." He patted Meg's shoulder. "Thanks, honey, for the use of your deck."

"Say good night to the Evanses, Peter," Mrs. Dawson said. "We've a long drive and had better get started."

Peter looked at Meg. For a moment his eyes held hers. They understood, both of them, that the other didn't want to say good-bye, that they both hoped they'd soon see each other again.

Peter's mother said, "Come along, Peter. We've had a lovely evening but we must go now."

Peter cringed at the summons, but there was no other way than for him to follow his parents down the boarding ladder. Meg watched him as long as she could, but the Dawsons and Whitelocks were soon swallowed by darkness.

"Tyler!" Aunt Lavinia called. "Are you comin' down here where we can talk normal, or must I shout?"

"We're comin', Aunt Lavinia," Meg said with a sigh.

Mr. Evans followed Meg. The others hastily disappeared belowdecks like rabbits into a warren.

"Hello, Aunt Lavinia, Uncle Lester," Meg said. "You should see how nice Dad's made the *Tessie!* Won't you change your mind and come aboard?"

"Up that ladder?" Aunt Lavinia's voice squeaked. "When I left Smith Island twenty years ago to marry your Uncle Lester, young lady, I promised myself never to set foot on a Bay boat again. I had more than enough of that foolishness while I was a girl! No. I just came to see with my own eyes if it could be true that your father had crowded his family onto an old boat. I want to urge you, Tyler, beg you to reconsider."

"I don't know, Vinny. I admit it's unusual, but we— well, the house had been sold, and I couldn't seem t'find another place near my work. It seemed a good answer for the time bein'."

"You could've come to Cambridge."

"But Aunt Lavinia, we love the *Tessie!*" Meg blurted out. "Us kids begged Dad to fix her up and let us live on her!"

"Well, be that as it may, a boatyard's no place to raise a family, especially a child as young as Kathy. Runnin' around the docks she could fall in and drown!"

"She doesn't run around the docks 'less someone older's keepin' an eye on her," Meg said.

"And livin' cramped together in the hull of that old boat. It can't be healthy! Where is Kathy, by the way? Where is my baby?"

"In bed."

"In bed? You mean in *bunk*, or maybe swingin' in a hammock like a common sailor! We could put her in the back seat, Lester, where she'd go on sleepin'. Let me take her, Tyler, before somethin' happens you'll regret. Meg means well, but she's too young to be responsible for a small child. In a fix she'd go all t'pieces, not have the maturity to handle an emergency. Let us take Kathy before it's too late."

"Now, Vinnie—" Tyler began.

"Lavinia, we'd better go along," Uncle Lester interrupted. "It's late, and there's nothin' we can do about your brother's family tonight. They're livin' as they see fit. Let's go." He took her arm.

She moved reluctantly toward the car but didn't stop talking. "It appears I'm bein' taken home, Tyler, but I'll be back. And when I come, I'll bring a caseworker from the Children's Bureau. They look into cases of child neglect. She can judge if Kathy's sufferin' for lack of a mature person t'look after her and from substandard livin' conditions!"

With this parting thrust she climbed into the car and slammed the door. Uncle Lester got in on the other side. He swung the car around and drove away.

Meg was trembling with rage. "Why does she do things like that, Dad?"

Her father shook his head wearily. "She just takes notions, I reckon. Always has. Can't stand t'let well enough alone."

"Will she really try to take Kathy away again?"

"Prob'ly. But she won't be able to."

"I hope you're right," Meg said as they turned to go up the ladder. Privately, she was not so sure.

135

13

IN THE DAYS that followed, Meg was regularly the first one to reach the mailbox after the postman arrived. Peter had said nothing about writing, but Meg was hopeful. On the other hand, the sound of tires grating on gravel gave her a sinking feeling in her stomach. She worried that Aunt Lavinia would make good her threat and drop in one day accompanied by some stern person from the Cambridge Children's Bureau. But several weeks passed without a sign of her aunt or a word from Peter. She wondered if he'd gone to Maine.

Scaredy was still missing. At one time or another each

member of the family had tried hard to find her. Mr. Evans had gone back to their old house to see if she had somehow made her way there. Meg had walked along the blacktop calling and searching. Secretly she feared Scaredy had met her end, as so many small furry things did, under the wheels of a car. Kathy hadn't forgotten her kitten.

One evening in late July Mr. Evans lingered at the table with his cup of tea while Lloyd and Meg were washing and drying the dishes. Jamie was scribbling in a lined notebook. He was still determined to trap muskrats as soon as the fall season opened and was already figuring his profits. Kathy snuggled up to her father and said in a mournful voice, "No more Scaredy, Daddy. I miss her lots!"

Mr. Evans drained his cup of tea. "I know where there are plenty of Scaredys. On Smith Island. Every house has two or three hangin' around, not t'mention the half-wild ones that scrounge about the docks after fish leavin's. There's no easy way for cats to get off the island, and nothin' there t'keep their numbers down, so they just multiply."

"That's what I'm tryin' t'do," Jamie said. "Somehow it don't come out right. Dad, why did you leave Smith Island?"

" 'Cause my fingers itched for the feel of good tools and fine wood. I never cared much for handlin' wet nets and haulin' crab traps. Boat buildin' come so natural—"

"Daddy," Kathy asked, "can we get 'nudder Scaredy? Can we?"

"How about a pet crab, Kat?" Jamie asked. "I caught one today you might like. He's big as a kitten and a lovely shade of blue."

"No, no, no! Don't want pinchy old crab!"

"Jamie's just teasing," Meg said. "James, how about taking out this trash? Come on, Kathy. It's time for bed."

The next morning Lloyd packed himself a lunch of peanut butter sandwiches, a Coke, cookies, and an apple in a paper bag and started out once more to hike to Meekins Neck. He knew the goose's nest would be long gone, but he was curious to see what changes had taken place. The sky was overcast. Just as well, Lloyd thought. It could be hot as blazes on the blacktop in July when the sun was trying its hardest.

Lloyd expected changes and he found them. Small white stakes marked future homesites along a semicircular road thirty feet wide with concrete curbs. Large culverts drained the former marshland, dumping the fresh water loaded with topsoil into the Honga. Lloyd walked along the road kicking now and then at the ugly curb, until he came to the spot where the goose's nest had been. It was now in someone's freshly sodded backyard. He sat on the curb and ate his lunch. It didn't taste like much. He crumpled the brown paper bag savagely and thrust it into his pocket. Then he walked on around toward the blacktop. He saw few wild creatures compared with the numbers that used to make the marsh their home—only a couple of crows, some squirrels, and the ever-present buzzards flying high. That was all. Before he completed the semicircle, it began to rain—a miserable, insistent drizzle. He walked faster, with shoulders hunched and head down. When he reached the blacktop, he turned toward home.

He didn't raise his head at the swish of tires behind him until he heard brakes. Looking up he saw that a pickup truck had pulled off onto the shoulder. It had the insignia of the Blackwater Wildlife Refuge, a circled wild goose in flight, painted on its door.

The driver rolled down his window. "How about a lift?" he asked.

When Lloyd saw the driver's face close up, his own brightened. "Thanks a lot, Mr. Prior," he said. "This rain isn't much for walkin'." He climbed in. "I guess you don't remember me. There were so many kids that day!" He took off his glasses, which were misted over, to dry them.

As Mr. Prior pulled out onto the highway again, he dug into his memory searching for a name to put to this boy's face. "Lloyd . . . Lloyd Hughes?" he ventured.

"Lloyd Evans. My class was from the Fishing Creek School. We visited Blackwater last spring."

"Now I remember. That was the day we saw the duck with an arrow through his rear end."

"Poor old duck! Did you ever find him?"

"No, more's the pity, or the archer either. Don't you have a sister who likes to sketch birds?"

Lloyd grinned. "That's Meg. She won a prize for a sea gull sketch once. She's been too busy to sketch much lately. You see—" Lloyd hesitated. It was such a long story. "We've moved."

"A good move, I hope."

"Yes, that part of it's good."

After a pause Mr. Prior said, "I came down to take a look at an oil slick that's been reported on the beach near Hoopersville. Also, I want to try to find out more about some poaching that's been going on in this area."

"There was some shooting when I was here in June."

"D'you know where it came from?"

Lloyd didn't know what to say. He didn't like being a teller of tales. Then he thought of the gander plummeting into the river and the goose alone on her nest, and his remembered anger made him want to tell what little he knew. "The shooting came from that big blind just north of the new subdivision. There were men and a dog. They took some ducks and . . . and a wild goose."

"Doesn't surprise me. That farm's owned by a fellow from Cambridge named Messick. He's not particular who uses his blinds or when. I've had my eye on him for some time."

Lloyd felt relieved, somehow, that someone else knew about Uncle Lester. "There was a nest with eggs. We found it in May and saved it from being bulldozed. I checked up on it every now and then till the goslings hatched. That day the gander was shot. I don't know if the old goose managed to raise the goslings or not. The nest is long gone now."

"It was over there where they're building the subdivision?"

"Yes."

Mr. Prior glanced across the cab of the truck at Lloyd. "It's hard, isn't it, watching wild things hurt and natural beauty disappear."

"If I could just *do* something!" Lloyd exploded.

"I know how you feel. All conservationists feel the same way. But just keeping your eyes open and being aware of what's going on sometimes does a lot of good."

"I don't see how."

"Well, some folks just don't think. They're not deliberately setting out to destroy a marsh. It just gets in the way of what they're doing, and so it has to go."

"It's not right."

"No, it isn't. But the more people we have around like you who do care, the better. Sometimes opening people's eyes through education helps."

"What about hunters who kill out of season? They're pretty deliberate."

"That's where I come in," Mr. Prior said grimly.

The truck slowed and stopped in the line of cars waiting for the Honga bridge to close. For a minute the only sounds were the grinding of windshield wipers and the whispering rain.

Then Mr. Prior said, "So you've moved. Where d'you live now?

"We're living on a boat, an old bugeye that's been beached."

"That's unusual. Where is she?"

"In Whitelock's Boatyard."

"I know where that is. I'll be going right by there. I can drop you off. And maybe you'd let me take a look at your new—uh, home. I'd be real interested."

When they reached the boatyard, Mr. Prior parked the truck, and they ran through the rain to the *Tessie.* He followed Lloyd down the companionway into the cabin, where Meg was hammering away on a frame she was making for one of her sketches.

"Meg, this is Mr. Prior. He wanted to see the *Tessie.*"

Meg smiled. She liked the look of the young man in the olive drab Ranger's uniform with his peaked cap at such a jaunty angle. "Welcome aboard, Mr. Prior. Lloyd's told me about you." She held out her hand, and his clasp was warm and friendly.

"Lloyd told me about you, too, and I remembered. You

sketch birds. I helped judge the wildlife contest at your school last spring." He glanced at the picture beside her. "May I see? A pair of ospreys, right?"

"Uh, huh. We saw them going down the Honga. They nest on top of those channel markers, you know."

Mr. Prior studied the sketch. "You sure have an eye for detail. The markings are remarkably accurate. Do you have others here?"

Meg rummaged around and found more sketches tucked away in a pile of school books and papers. Mr. Prior looked them over carefully.

"Would you let me borrow several to exhibit at the Information Center at Blackwater? I think they'd add a lot to our display."

"You really think they're good enough for that?" Meg's face glowed with pleasure.

"I do. I especially like your ospreys, and this gull on the wing has real style."

"I hope someday I'll get a chance to sketch a swan. I can't think of anything more lovely to look at than a swan!"

"Have you heard about the new stunt we're trying with swan?"

"No. Tell us about it." Lloyd said.

"Well, everyone knows about banding birds as a way of studying migration habits, but with swan number 237 we tried something new. He carried a radio transmitter on his back which broadcast a pulsing sound that could be picked up on the ground or in aircraft. Our hope was to track him to his nesting grounds in northern Canada."

"A radio? Wouldn't that be too heavy for a bird to carry?" Meg asked.

"Not 237. We chose him for his size and spunk, and

the radio we used weighed only four ounces. It had an antenna nearly a foot long that concerned us some, but it didn't seem to bother him."

"And were you able to track him?" Lloyd asked.

"For a way. The weather didn't help. He flew north to Annapolis, then into Pennsylvania, where he was forced down by a March blizzard. A chase plane had been following him but had to turn back, so we kept track of him from the ground. After the storm he continued on to Rondeau Park, Ontario, touched down on Lake St. Clair, Michigan, then continued west to North Dakota, where he joined a flock of about 24,000 other swans. Unfortunately, we lost him after that because of a lack of tracking equipment north of the border at that point. Next spring we hope to do better."

"Is 237 saddled with that radio and antenna forever?" Meg asked.

"No. The body harness is made of material that deteriorates in about three months and falls off."

"Mr. Prior," Lloyd asked earnestly, "if I wanted t'be a wildlife manager like you, how should I go about it?"

"Study all the natural sciences you can. You could work as a volunteer at Blackwater in your spare time. After you're a bit older, perhaps you could get a summer job. Then you'd want to go to the University. There are scholarships, you know, if money's a problem." He looked at his watch. "I've gotta get goin'! I'll take good care of your sketches, Meg."

Soon after Mr. Prior left, Jamie came up from the dock proudly displaying a good-sized rockfish. "Caught your supper, Meg," he said.

"That's fine, Jamie. But would you be extra nice and clean it, too?"

With a shrug he started back to the dock, but he met his father headed toward the *Tessie*. He sensed something unusual had happened and reversed his course. The others gathered around them.

"Called your Uncle Fred on Smith Island," Mr. Evans said. "He's urgin' us t'come visit for the weekend."

"Fantabulous!" Jamie exclaimed. "I've always wanted t'go to Smith Island!"

"Me, too," Meg said. "I want t'see the place where you grew up, Dad."

"Scaredy-cats! Scaredy-cats! I want a Scaredy-cat!" Kathy chanted.

"I want to go fishing," said Lloyd.

"Can we go, Dad?" Meg asked. "It would be great fun!"

"Don't reckon I oughtta leave the boatyard on a summer weekend with all the boatin' folk comin' in and all—"

The young Evanses' faces fell.

"But there's no reason you all can't go. You need a vacation anyway. So your Uncle Fred's comin' for you in his crabber tomorrow mornin' after he unloads his crabs in Crisfield. You'll like spendin' some time with your Aunt Alice. She's a real fine woman."

Meg agreed it would be nice to see Aunt Alice again. She was also thinking it would be mighty pleasant not having to worry about Aunt Lavinia for three whole days!

14

MEG WOKE VERY EARLY her first morning on Smith Island. For the most part the
windows were still black, but the beam from
a street light came through one to make
sharp shadows on the bedroom wall. She had been awakened by the sound of car engines starting up, rough as
outboard motors, here and there all over town. Smith Island crabbers were heading for their boats. They made
it a habit to be out on the Bay before daylight. This morning Lloyd and Jamie would be going out with Uncle
Fred. Meg had declined the invitation; she was too glad

to be able to sleep late. She snuggled gratefully down beside Kathy. But it was a while before she slept. She could hear the hollow sound of the local foghorn, ah-uhh, ah-uhh, on the navigation light down by the waterway, and the hum of the huge generator down the street that supplied all the island's electricity. She was drifting off, when the yowl of a lovesick cat under the window brought her wide awake again. At last, counting the seconds between the soundings of the horn, she went to sleep.

When she woke again, sunshine was streaming through the ruffled curtains at the windows, and Kathy was patting her head. " 'S morning, Meggie. Time t'get up!"

Meg groaned. "Go 'way, Kathy, and let me sleep."

"But it's morning!"

"Go downstairs and find Aunt Alice," Meg mumbled grumpily.

Kathy slipped out of bed, and Meg heard her patter down the stairs. Sounds came up from the kitchen. Tommy and Timmy, Aunt Alice's twins, must be up too, she decided, before she drifted off to sleep again.

Suddenly, she was jolted awake by a voice that was unmistakably Uncle Fred's. Uncle Fred? Uncle Fred had left with Lloyd and Jamie hours ago! Curiosity overcame sleepiness, and she sat up in bed. Uncle Fred was saying, "It's flat calm today. Hardly a breath movin'. It's mighty hot! The girls up yet? Over."

Meg heard a click. Then Aunt Alice was saying, "Kathy's havin' breakfast with the boys, but Meg's still sleepin'. She doesn't often get a chance to sleep in the mornin', I dare say. How's your catch?"

There was another click, and Uncle Fred's voice came again. "Middlin'. I've ten, twelve bushel and another forty traps to empty. One trap was full of sea nettles. Stung my hands pretty bad. It's good havin' the boys along. I'll keep in touch. Over and out."

Meg realized she'd been listening to a ship-to-shore radio.

The bathroom in Aunt Alice's house was downstairs. Meg took her towel and toothbrush and started down. She found Aunt Alice in front of the stove scrambling eggs. She was a small, birdlike woman with quick hands and beady black eyes that crinkled when she laughed. Kathy sat at the kitchen table eating toast and jelly, enjoying the attention of her cousins. She was telling them about her lost kitten. "She was white and gray with a big fluffy tail, this big!" Her hands measured the imagined size of the kitten.

"Mornin', Aunt Alice."

"Mornin', Meg. Sleep well?" An amused glint shone in her eyes. "Kathy's been entertainin' the boys. Scaredy? That the name of her missin' kitten?"

"Uh-huh, and she'd sure like another to take her place!"

"Well, now, let's see. There's plenty of cats 'round here, but we'd have t'look some t'find a kitten that's just right for Kathy. By the way, how'd you like to go over to Tylerton this mornin'? It's a curious, out-of-the-way place, and I'd like you t'take a look in Guy Pruitt's woodworkin' shop. Who knows? We just might find a kitten."

"We'd like that fine, Aunt Alice."

"Someone's bound t'be goin' that way can give us a lift," she continued, putting generous portions of scrambled eggs on everyone's plate. "The only way t'get there's by boat. I'll take the boys next door to cousin Millie's. They're not much for excursions."

An hour later Aunt Alice, Meg, and Kathy stood on the deck of the *Stella* in a crescent of shade made by her

147

cabin. The *Stella* was a heavy-built fishing boat used sometimes for delivering freight between the mainland and Smith Island. She chugged along sedately, passing docks, fishing shanties, storage shacks, and the many small white frame houses that made up the town of Ewell. When they reached Tangier Sound, her captain turned south, skirting the island but staying well offshore since the area was shallow and the *Stella* drew a good bit of water. Rounding a marshy point, he steered her into Tyler's Creek, where the channel was deep right up to the docks. As they came in close, Kathy spotted a scrawny, half-grown kitten sniffing around the trash barrels on the wharf.

"A Scaredy-cat! A Scaredy-cat!" she cried. Holding onto the rail to keep her balance, she jumped up and down with excitement.

But before the *Stella* was secured at the dock, the kitten had scampered off.

"We'll find another," Meg said.

"A better-lookin' one, I should hope!" Aunt Alice laughed.

They went into the General Store, where Aunt Alice nodded to everyone. The customers were in no hurry to make their purchases and depart, but took time to visit. A retired waterman sat reading a newspaper in one of the dilapidated lounge chairs provided for that purpose. Two more men sat at a card table in the corner playing checkers.

Aunt Alice bought the girls ice cream cones. Licking around the edges to keep the ice cream from dripping, they walked down the shady main street on their way to visit Guy Pruitt's woodworking shop. The small houses they passed had ruffled white curtains at their windows and gardens tucked around the houses like flowered quilts. Along the low picket fences hollyhocks stood tall, their blossoms marching up sturdy green stalks with leaves as big as water-lily pads.

The door to Guy Pruitt's woodworking shop stood open, but he was nowhere about. His towheaded grandson, who was playing ball nearby, offered to go for him. While they waited, Meg examined Mr. Pruitt's workshop, a lean-to attached to the shop. It smelled of freshly sawn wood, and sawdust lay everywhere. It clung to the spider webs around the windows, ran in rivulets on the concrete floor, and lay in a small pile beside the workbench. On top of the workbench, chisels and knives were neatly laid out beside an electric saw. Cans of paint and glue stood on a shelf above. Chunks of wood of a size for carving were stacked away in corners of the room.

"Howdy, Alice," Mr. Pruitt said, stepping into the workshop. He was a tall, thin man, a little stooped, with snowy hair and keen blue eyes under bushy brows. "Johnny says you want to see my carvings." He unlocked the door to his showroom.

Inside, Meg saw carved water birds of all sizes and species arranged on shelves that lined the walls. There were mallards, canvasbacks, wood ducks, black ducks, pintails, and blue-winged teals. Besides the ducks, Mr. Pruitt had carvings of Canada geese, gulls, and sandpipers. There was a handsome bas-relief of geese on the wing and an exquisite small carving of a wild swan with its wing extended and its long neck curved as though preening feathers. Meg was enchanted.

"Mr. Pruitt," she asked, "how long did it take you to learn to carve like this?" She had picked up the swan and was studying it carefully.

"A lot o' years," he replied. "I started when I was a boy carvin' decoys for hunters." He had a faraway look in his eyes. "It's harder than you might think to fool a wild bird, but I got pretty good at it. Finally, I grew tired of birds sittin' lifeless in the water, wings tight to their bodies, and began tryin' my hand at birds on the wing. A bird's wing is wondrously made!"

"I can see that." Meg still held the swan lovingly. "I've done some sketches of water birds, but seeing this makes me realize how much I still have to learn."

"Don't begrudge time taken in learnin'. If you've talent and keep tryin', you'll be rewarded in the end."

"If I could draw as well as you carve, Mr. Pruitt, I wouldn't care how long it took t'learn."

"She has real talent, Guy," Aunt Alice said. "I've seen some of her work."

"Next time you visit your aunt let me have a look. Mebbe I'd have a suggestion or two for you."

"That would be wonderful! Drawing's awfully important to me. It makes me—feel like I'm using myself the way I want to. It's hard to explain. I like doing lots of other things, too. But the good feeling I get if I draw something, and it turns out all right, is best of all."

Mr. Pruitt looked at her with sympathy. "I understand just what you're sayin', young lady."

"Meg, I'll try t'see you have a chance to come again. Meanwhile, I b'lieve I'll take that little sandpiper, Guy. He's real perky. Then we'd better start back."

Kathy tugged at Mr. Pruitt's sleeve. "D'you have any Scaredy-cats?"

"No, honey," he said puzzled. "I don't carve cats. Just birds."

"She's talking about a live kitten, Mr. Pruitt," Meg explained.

They returned to Ewell by a shortcut through the marsh. A young man named Joe was going back up the island in his outboard motorboat, and he offered them a ride.

"Mr. Pruitt's really a good artist, isn't he?" Meg turned to her aunt as they settled themselves into the boat.

Aunt Alice grinned. "I *thought* you'd enjoy meetin' old Guy, bein' so creative yourself and all. You do what he says, and bring some of your pictures next time you come. Or mail him some when you get home."

"I will."

"Your daddy's mighty proud of your drawin'; he told us about the display at the Wildlife Refuge. He wants you t'keep it up. And I do, too."

Meg looked at her aunt in surprise. She hadn't realized that the family had been discussing her.

Aunt Alice continued. "Much as your daddy and the kids need you now, Meg, nobody means for you to forget your drawin'. *Make* time for it. It's a God-given gift."

"Yes'm, I know. I will." Meg smiled her agreement. Aunt Alice certainly was a welcome change from Aunt Lavinia.

Smith Island was quiet on Sunday mornings. No noisy cars took men to their boats before dawn. No chugging crab boats followed the Thoroughfare out onto the Bay. There were church bells, but they came later.

Aunt Alice went to church early. She was the choir director and the church organist, and she went in time to rehearse her choir before the congregation arrived. Uncle Fred rounded up the rest of the family and got them to church soon after the bells rang for service. They all sat in the family pew up front. The service was lengthy, and Kathy slipped down onto the floor during the sermon and crawled under the pews to look at people's shoes. Meg didn't succeed in getting her back until the final hymn.

Church was followed by Aunt Alice's traditional Sunday dinner—fried chicken, mashed potatoes, and corn on the cob. Meg was sure when she saw the heaping platters that Aunt Alice would have leftovers for a week, but Jamie and Lloyd did their share, and Uncle Fred's appetite was substantial. All during the meal Timmy and Tommy wriggled on their chairs, poked each other in the ribs, looked at each other and then at Kathy, and giggled. Finally, Aunt Alice excused them from the table.

Uncle Fred pushed his chair back and loosened his belt.

Aunt Alice said, "We'll have dessert in the back yard. More of the family and some friends are comin' over." Still she made no move to leave the table.

The screen door in the kitchen banged, and Timmy and Tommy came in looking like well-matched imps. They carried a picnic basket between them.

Timmy said, "It's for Kathy."

"For Kathy," Tommy said.

They put the basket on the floor beside Kathy. She looked at it suspiciously.

"Open it, lollipop," Meg said.

Kathy slid off her chair and lifted the lid of the basket. "A Scaredy-cat!" she squealed.

Inside the basket lay a gray and white kitten with a fluffy tail, a kitten just the right size for a little girl's pet. Kathy lifted her from the basket by her middle and cuddled her close under her chin.

"That's a real nice kitten," Meg said. "What d'you say, Kathy?"

"T'ank you, Timmy and Tommy."

The twins smirked.

"Not a bad-lookin' cat," Jamie said, coming around the table. "I'll trade you my pet crab."

"No, no, no!" Kathy said.

"She looks just like Scaredy number one," Lloyd said.

"Let's go out back and play," Timmy said. "Bring the cat."

"Bring the cat, and you come too," said Tommy.

Uncle George, Aunt Martha, and their six children arrived just as Meg and Aunt Alice were finishing the dinner dishes. Aunt Martha took an apron down from the wall to help. Her oldest child, George, Junior, had a box under his arm with holes punched in the top. "Where's Kathy?" he asked.

"She and the twins are out back." Meg went out onto the porch with him. "Kathy!" she called, "Come here! Cousin George wants to see you."

Kathy came running, followed by the twins. George handed her his box. She put it down on the porch steps and pulled off the lid. Inside was a yellow kitten, fluffy as a dandelion. Kathy was enchanted. "Two Scaredy-cats!" she murmured blissfully.

George's face fell. "Two? Guess someone else beat me to it. It was yesterday I heard she needed one, but it took some looking t'find one that was just right."

Seeing his disappointment Meg said, "Maybe we can use two."

At that moment cousins Mark and Joanne came through the house looking secretive, their hands behind their backs.

"Hi, Kathy!" Mark said.

"Hi, Kathy!" Joanne said. "We've got somethin' for you."

Kathy looked at them bewildered. Meg sighed.

Slowly Mark and Joanne brought their hands from behind their backs. In each hand lay a tiny kitten, eyes still closed.

"They're for you, Kathy!" Joanne said.

"You dopes!" their older brother said. "You've stolen Topsy's kittens. They're too young. You oughtta know that!"

"Kathy can have Topsy *and* her kittens," Joanne said. "Mommy wouldn't mind."

"No! Oh, no!" Meg exclaimed. "You're good kids, but that's too many kittens! You'd better take Topsy's babies back to her before she gets worried."

Just then Aunt Alice came out onto the porch carrying a tray loaded with plates and fresh peach pies. Uncle Fred followed her with an ice cream freezer. "Who wants t'turn the crank?" he asked.

More people had gathered in the Evanses' back yard—old people, young people, in-betweens, and children. By the time each child had a turn cranking the ice cream freezer, the cream had thickened. Uncle Fred tried the crank. He could hardly move it, and declaring the ice cream done, he removed the top, carefully wiped the coarse salt from the lid of the cannister, and took it off. He lifted the beater high for all to see. Gobs of ice cream, golden vanilla, clung to it. "Lloyd and Jamie have the first lick," he said. "They're visitors."

The children passed pieces of peach pie with dollops of ice cream on top. Groups settled on the grass all over the yard to enjoy it. Meg looked up from her plate to see her Aunt Mary coming out of the kitchen door. She jumped up and ran to meet her.

Aunt Mary taught school on the island. In her spare

time she wrote about the island's early history. She was tall and slender, with short, wheat-colored hair that had a windblown look. Her eyes were deep blue and wise. They shone with pleasure when she saw Meg. "I hear you've moved onto a marvelous old bugeye! Tell me about her."

"Let me get you some pie 'n ice cream," Meg said. "Then we'll find a place where we can talk."

They sat on the grass in a quiet corner of the yard. As Aunt Mary dug her fork in, Meg said, "We love livin' on the *Tessie*. Dad's fixed her up so she's real comfortable. She makes me feel as if—as if she wants t'help keep the family together. If only—" She looked searchingly at her aunt, wondering if she should go on.

"If only what?" Aunt Mary's eyes were sympathetic.

"If only Aunt Lavinia would leave us alone! How can sisters be so different?"

"So Lavinia's still pestering you about Kathy?"

"She wants Kathy real bad."

"Well, Kathy's a charmer all right. But she belongs with you and your father."

"I wish Aunt Lavinia believed that! She means t'bring a social worker down t'look us over! Can she make us give Kathy up, if the social worker says to?"

"I don't know. Lester swings a good deal of weight in Dorchester County. He's in a position to do favors and usually goes along with what Lavinia wants."

"Ever since the Fourth of July I've been scared every time I heard a car in the driveway."

"But she hasn't come?"

Meg shook her head.

"Maybe she's having a difficult time persuading the agency Kathy's as badly off as she makes out. Or she may be waiting till near time school begins to make her move.

155

Perhaps I can talk to her. We've grown apart since she left the island but . . . Come to think of it, I need to go to Easton anyway. Maybe I could have a talk with Lavinia, then swing down to Hooper's and have a visit with your dad, God love him!"

"That would be great, Aunt Mary!"

That evening Meg was in the kitchen helping Aunt Alice. Kathy and the twins raced from one end of the house to the other after the kittens. Uncle Fred settled himself at the kitchen table with a cold beer. "Get your dad t'come back to the island, Meg. There lots of folks would like t'see him do that!"

"Dad needs boats t'build, Uncle Fred."

"A man's got t'be practical too. Livin' on the old *Tessie's* all right durin' the summer, but what will y'all do come winter?"

"If Dad puts in a shipmate stove, I think we'd be all right. Her sides are good and tight. The portholes fit like corks."

"You'd be real cozy in a little house here," Aunt Alice said. "I'd be glad to look after Kathy while your dad was out on the Bay and you were away at school. She'd be company for Timmy and Tommy."

"Away at school? You mean real far away?"

"On the main. We've no high school here. The kids take the *Island Star* each Monday and come back Friday after school. They say it's the only school boat in the country. The Islanders stay with families in Crisfield during the week. The state pays their board."

"I wouldn't like being away from the family all week."

"A lotta kids feel that way at first, but they get used to it. Lloyd and Jamie could go to school on the island. I expect they pretty much look after themselves."

Kathy had captured the yellow kitten, and the twins were squabbling over the other.

"Time you three went to bed!" Uncle Fred said. "I'll take them up, Alice. You've had a long day. Kids, put the kittens in their basket on the back porch and come with me."

After the children were on their way to bed, Meg said, "Aunt Alice, you're real kind, you and Uncle Fred, wantin' us to live here. You *do* understand about Dad and his boats, don't you? That's his trade, and he's skillful. We can't take that away from him, 'specially now." She didn't tell her aunt the other thing that bothered her. There was too much family on Smith Island! All those cousins, uncles, and aunts! If they moved to the island, young as she was, they'd all be telling her what to do!

She was drying the last plate, and Aunt Alice was wiping off the sink, when the front doorbell rang. They heard Uncle Fred talking to someone. Together they walked to the front of the house. There they saw Mr. Pruitt's grandson, Johnny, standing by the front door. Kathy sat on the bottom step of the stairs with a box on her lap. She laboriously undid the fancy yellow ribbon tied around it and took off the lid. A calico kitten sprang from the box, looked around with frightened eyes, then scampered under the sofa in the living room.

Meg sat down weakly on the stair beside Kathy. "No, oh no!" she gasped.

"But I thought you needed one!" Johnny said, looking from Kathy to Meg, bewildered.

"That was yesterday!" Meg said.

15

WHEN UNCLE FRED dropped the young Evanses off at the boatyard on Monday afternoon, they found their father working on a stranger, a long sleek yacht named *Wind Mistress.*

"She's a sick one all right!" Mr. Evans said. "Spots of dry rot soft as 'n old potato! She needs a lotta work, and there's not much time t'do it in. Her owners have entered her in the Solomons Island race on Labor Day."

"What has t'be done, Dad?" Meg asked.

"I'll have t'take a big chunk of infected wood outta her keel and replace it with clean. All her members will have t'be treated with wood preserver. That's one advantage the new glass boats have—no dry rot. Still, I like wood better."

Meg looked at the mail and found a postcard from Peter Dawson mailed in Maine. On the front was a picture of a fishing schooner under full sail, bounding bravely over bright blue waves topped by white foam. Meg read the message several times. It said, "We drove up here in Jeff Smith's VW, so I didn't have to hitch after all. This is great country, but no jobs so far. Wish you were here. Love, Peter."

Love, Peter? Did that mean *love*, or was it just a usual way of signing off? The question plagued her. Then she let her imagination take over, and she and Peter were together again. Sometimes he was taking a stint at the helm of the schooner, his hands firmly on the wheel and his head thrown back. She stood beside him. At other times he was with her on the *Tessie*, watching as she moved easily about the ship, smiling his lop-sided grin. She wondered when he'd ever come back.

The morning after they got back, Meg and Kathy set out to mail some sketches to Mr. Pruitt and to return a casserole dish to Mrs. Whitelock. It had held a crab pie which Mrs. Whitelock had sent over to their father while they were gone. The grass was slippery because it had rained during the night. Kathy scampered on ahead, but Meg walked carefully. All at once, she felt a sharp pain in her foot. Thrown off balance, she stumbled, slipped on the grass, and to her horror dropped the casserole dish, which broke in two. She sat down on the wet grass and took off her sneaker. A nail in a bit of wood hidden in the grass had pierced the sole and bloodied her foot. It hurt, but she didn't mind that as much as breaking the dish. How could she tell Mrs. Whitelock?

Kathy came running back. "Oh, oh, Meggie! Dish all broken!"

"Oh, be quiet!" Meg said crossly. Her foot hurt, and the dish was done for. She looked guiltily toward the house, wondering if anyone had witnessed her accident. She was tempted to remove the evidence and retreat hastily to the *Tessie*. Then she realized that wouldn't save her from explanations. Thoroughly shaken, she picked up the pieces and went on.

Going through the gate in the picket fence, they heard the old lady talking to someone. Meg tapped on the screen door to the kitchen, but no one came. Puzzled, they went around to the front of the house. There they found Mrs. Whitelock on her knees in front of her flowers talking to her petunias. "Well, that soakin' did you good. Given a little rain to wash your faces, you look up smilin'!"

"Hi, Mis' Witock," Kathy said. "Meg broke your dish!"

Mrs. Whitelock sat back on her heels, pushed her glasses back onto the bridge of her nose, and looked at Meg severely. "Well, now, how'd you come t'do that? I was fond of that dish."

"I stepped on a nail and slipped. It broke in two pieces. Maybe it could be glued back together again."

"Don't hardly think so."

"Well, could we get you another?"

"It's a special kind they've got in California. My daughter-in-law sent it to me for my birthday."

"Oh, dear. That really makes me feel bad! Isn't there

anything we can do 'bout it, Mrs. Whitelock? I'm awfully sorry!" Meg was close to tears.

Seeing her distress, Mrs. Whitelock softened. "Well—accidents will happen. Let's forget it." She sighed. "A little of that weed pullin', and my back sure lets me know about it. Give me a hand gettin' to my feet, and we'll get rid of the wreckage."

Meg helped her up. Mrs. Whitelock smoothed her flowered apron down over her pants—an old pair of the captain's—and straightened her broad-brimmed garden hat. Patting Kathy on the head she said, "How about some cookies? They're fresh baked."

"Mm-m cookies!" Kathy said. "Mis' Witock—"

"I'd be glad for you t'call me somethin' else. How 'bout Gramma Bessie?"

"That's nice. Gramma Bessie, would you like t'see my new Scaredy-cat?" Kathy had agreed, under protest, to leave all but one of the kittens with her cousins.

" 'Deed I would! Go get her and we'll give her some milk. Or would she like a cookie?"

"You funny, Gramma Bessie. Kitties don't like cookies!"

The summer was going fast, too fast. So far the Evanses had been spared a visit from Aunt Lavinia, but Meg felt certain she'd show up eventually. If only they had a plan for Kathy's care in the fall! But neither she nor her father had been able to find a solution. Meg even thought of dropping out of school. If Dad would only agree to write a hardship letter . . . Then she remembered her friends and the sketching course she'd been looking forward to. Dad was right. She didn't want to be a dropout.

On a stifling day soon after the first of August, the marine supplier called from Cambridge to say that their long-awaited sink had arrived.

"I'll borrow the pickup and go to Cambridge right away," Mr. Evans said while they were having lunch. "Lloyd, you'd better come along and help load the crate."

The truck hadn't been gone fifteen minutes when Meg heard another set of tires on the driveway. Coming topsides, she saw a small car drive slowly past the boatyard office and stop. The door opened, and Aunt Mary stepped out, looking fresh and flowerlike.

In her hurry Meg half slid down the boarding ladder. "Aunt Mary!" she exclaimed, hugging her hard. "It's so good t'see you!"

"It's good to see you, too, Meg. You look fine, brown as a berry and twice as pretty. Hello there, Miss Kathy!" she added as Kathy came tagging along.

"How's everything going for you?" Meg asked. "How're things on Smith Island?"

"Timmy and Tommy came down with measles the week after you left. Otherwise all is well. Where's your dad?"

Meg gulped. "Oh, Aunt Mary! What bad luck! He's gone to Cambridge. Left just a few minutes ago!"

"That *is* too bad! I did so want to see him!"

"He'll really be disappointed when he finds out you were here!"

"Get him to bring you out to the island, Meg. It's not a hard trip, you know. A short drive to Crisfield, then the ferry. Well, how about a tour of the *Tessie?*"

They climbed aboard, and Aunt Mary took a large pad of drawing paper and a set of felt marking pencils out of a paper bag and gave them to Kathy.

"Oh, Kathy! You'll have a lovely time with those. Take

them down to the table. That's a good place to draw,"
Meg suggested.

Rather listlessly, Kathy headed for the companionway.
Meg showed her aunt around the *Tessie*. Then they sat
on the forward deck, where the small amount of air coming off the bay made the heat more bearable.

"She's a great old ship, Meg!" Aunt Mary said. "Your
dad's done a masterful job of rebuilding her. He's saved
a member of an endangered species. D'you realize that?
These old working sailboats are in danger of becoming
extinct just like many of our birds and animals."

"I never thought of it that way," Meg said. "Did you
have a chance t'see Aunt Lavinia?"

"I did, and she's as stubborn as ever."

"How d'you mean?"

"Well, she's determined to have Kathy. Maintains it's
for Kathy's own good. Nothing I said budged her one
inch! She's just waiting for school to force you to make
a decision in her favor."

"But certainly a father has a right to his own child!"

"Yes, that's what one would think. But she's been talking to lawyers and social workers, pointing to your tender
years, your need to go to school, and your father's need
to work long and hard. Of course, they tell her what
she wants to hear. How about hiring some reliable woman
to stay with Kathy?"

"I asked Dad about that, and he thought it'd come too
dear. It takes a lotta money t'feed a family of five! Food's
costing more all the time. Soon we'll need winter clothes
and school books."

"Too bad there's not a good day-care center nearby. Is
there anyone you could leave her with?"

"I can't think of anyone."

Aunt Mary put her hand on her arm. "I wish I had some really splendid idea. But you know, my dear, I've a strong feeling you'll work it out. You're smart and you're determined. You'll find some better way of caring for Kathy than letting her go to Cambridge. Now, I must go or I'll miss the ferry back to the island. Give your dad my love."

Meg watched until the dust settled behind Aunt Mary's car. For all her kindness, she hadn't really helped. Heavyhearted, Meg went down the companionway into the cabin. To her surprise she found Kathy leaning on the table, her head in her arms.

"What's the matter, lollipop?"

"Don't feel good. Throat hurts."

Meg felt her forehead. It certainly was warm. But then, it was a very warm day. "Let's take a nap," she said. "You'll feel better after a nap."

When Kathy woke an hour or so later, her face was flushed, her throat still hurt, and she showed no interest in leaving her bunk. Meg wet a washcloth in cool water for her head and gave her a drink. She complained about the light hurting her eyes, so Meg drew the curtains over the portholes in their cabin.

Late in the afternoon Jamie came aboard. "Where is everyone?" he asked.

"Dad and Lloyd haven't come back from Cambridge," Meg said. "Kathy's sick."

"Gee, that's too bad. What's wrong with her?"

"She's feverish and has a sore throat."

"Well, I'm hungry. Do we have t'wait for Lloyd and Dad?"

"No. I'll fix something. I only wish Dad was here. I'm worried about Kathy and I don't know what t'do."

Kathy began coughing. "Meggie! Meggie! Throat hurts!" she cried.

"Mom used t'give us warm milk and honey for a sore throat," Jamie said. " 'Member?"

"We could try that, only I don't have any honey. I guess we could ask Mrs. Whitelock for some. Would you mind?"

"That old grouch?"

Jamie had had some trouble with Mrs. Whitelock about walking on her picket fence.

"She's not bad when you get to know her."

"Oh, all right."

While Jamie was gone, Meg fixed hot dogs. He returned with a jar of honey and some aspirin. Kathy couldn't swallow the aspirin, and the milk and honey made her throw up. Meg washed Kathy's face and laid a fresh cloth across her burning forehead. She wished desperately her father would come.

"I'm goin' t'look for night crawlers," Jamie said after they'd eaten. "Where's the flashlight?"

"In the drawer under Dad's bunk."

It began to grow dark outside. Meg sat beside Kathy, hoping all the while she'd soon hear the pickup returning. Kathy tossed and turned. When she coughed, she cried with pain. Meg tried singing to her and telling her stories, but the coughing spells came too frequently. When they subsided, Meg wiped her face and held a glass to her lips so that she could sip water. Every time Meg touched her, she felt hotter.

At last Kathy fell into a light sleep, though she still whimpered and moved about restlessly. Jamie came back, climbed into his bunk, and Meg lay down on hers. Why, oh why, doesn't Dad come? she asked herself.

Several hours later Meg was awakened by Kathy's hoarse cries. The cabin was black as pitch. Groggy with sleep, she felt her way into the main cabin, found the kerosene lamp, and lit it. To her dismay she saw that her father's bunk was still empty. She went back to Kathy, who was thrashing about crying, "Mama! Mama! I want my mama!"

Meg tried sponging her face and murmuring soothing words, but nothing calmed her.

"Mama!" she cried. "Hold me, Mama!"

Meg sat down, took her into her arms, and rocked her. Kathy's body was so hot it seemed as though she must melt.

"There, there, lollipop," Meg crooned. "Don't cry. Don't cry. It just makes your throat hurt worse."

Kathy's eyes flew open and she looked at Meg blankly with no sign of recognition in her eyes. She struggled to free herself of Meg's arms, then threw herself onto the bunk, thrashing around in a delirium.

Jamie stood in the door to the fo'c'sle rubbing his eyes. "What's goin' on? Where's Dad?" he asked.

"Wish I knew!" Meg said. "Jamie, we've got to get a doctor! Kathy's awful sick! Go wake the Whitelocks and ask Cap'n Noah to call Dr. Bounds. Quickly! I'm frightened!"

Without a word Jamie boosted himself out of the fo'c'sle hatch, and Meg heard his bare feet running across the deck. Then it was quiet except for Kathy's hoarse cries, her coughing and heavy breathing.

The minutes dragged slowly by, each one seeming an eternity. Meg felt utterly helpless. If only there were something she could do! She longed for her mother. She'd know how to ease Kathy's suffering. Meg bowed her head, and tears ran down her cheeks. She'd experienced death once this year. Was it to happen again? Dear God, she prayed, don't take Kathy! Please, please, dear God!

She felt a touch on her shoulder and raised her head to see Jamie, his boy's face filled with compassion. "Don't cry, Meggie. Cap'n Noah's called Dr. Bounds, and he's comin' right away. Cap'n Noah's goin' t'meet him at the end of the driveway so no time will be lost in findin' us. I'll wait with you till he comes."

Meg wiped the tears from her eyes, and Jamie sat down on the bunk beside her. "Mrs. Whitelock would've come over," he continued, "but she did something to her knee. It's so lame she can't manage the stairs."

"They're nice, both of them, Jamie."

"Lie down and rest a little, Meg. You're white as a sheet! I'll watch Kathy."

Obediently Meg stretched out on her bunk. Gradually, the sounds of Kathy's distress faded from her consciousness and she dozed. The next thing she knew, a man was speaking near her. She opened her eyes and saw Dr. Bounds bending over Kathy. The doctor was a huge bear of a man. His bulk nearly filled the space between her bunk and Kathy's. His bald head shone in the light from the kerosene lamp Captain Noah held high. To her relief she saw that her father and Lloyd were there too. Her father was leaning against the doorjamb, and she could see that his face was bruised and that he had a bump on his forehead.

"Open your mouth, sweetheart," Dr. Bounds was saying to Kathy, "and let me look at your throat."

In a few seconds he let her lie flat again. "It's a bad case! Worst I've seen in years. It's a good thing you dragged me out here, Captain, much as I dislike losin' my sleep!"

167

Meg sat up. "What's wrong with her, Dr. Bounds?"

"Measles. She has all the early symptoms. The rash will come."

"Will she—will she be all right?" Mr. Evans took hold of the doctor's arm.

"I hope so. She'll need good care. The trick is to avoid complications." He took a hypodermic needle from the black bag at his feet. "I'll give her a shot now. She'll be asleep in a minute." The doctor straightened up and turned to Mr. Evans. "Now Tyler, let's have a look at you."

They all filed out into the main cabin. Mr. Evans sat on his bunk while the doctor looked him over, turning his head this way and that and peering into his eyes. "Hurt here?"

Lloyd was on the bench by the table, his head in his arms. Meg slid in beside him. "What happened?" she whispered.

"Accident," he muttered without raising his head. "Tell you later."

Clearly Lloyd didn't want to explain anything at the moment, so Meg kept quiet. She was confused enough anyway. This whole night had an unreal, nightmarish quality.

Finally the doctor completed his examination of their father. "Where's your bed?"

"I'm sitting on it."

Meg helped Dr. Bounds arrange bedding for him, and at last Mr. Evans was able to lie down and settle his aching head on a pillow.

Now the doctor noticed Lloyd. "Son, let's have a look at you too, while we're at it."

Lloyd raised his head, and Meg noticed for the first

time that his face was bruised though not as badly as their father's. One of the lenses in his glasses was broken and the frames were bent out of shape.

After checking the bruises Dr. Bounds said, "You'll do. You'll have a shiner tomorrow, though, and you'll have to see an oculist."

"What about Dad?" Meg asked.

"He'll be plenty sore and he may have a slight concussion. But he'll be all right if he lies flat for a few days." He turned again to Lloyd. "Did the police bring you in, son?"

"Yes, after we walked into Honga."

"They'll fill out a report, then. You kids get to bed now. Meg, if Kathy wakes up, sponge her off with a damp cloth. Keeping the fever down is the important thing. I'll be back in the morning."

When the doctor was gone, Meg said to Lloyd, "You heard what the doctor said. Go to bed. It must be two o'clock."

"Three." His eye was beginning to swell shut.

"What happened? Was it a bad wreck?" She pulled him off the bench and steered him toward the fo'c'sle.

"Nah. We ran off the road. Only we didn't just run off." He paused, groggy from lack of sleep. "We were *forced* off, and I think I know who did it."

"Well, who?"

"Uncle Lester."

"Uncle Lester?"

"Yep." He stumbled on into the fo'c'sle. Jamie had long since found his bunk. Now Meg heard Lloyd fall into his, mumbling, "Good ole Uncle Lester."

For a while after Meg went back to bed, she lay awake wondering about what Lloyd had said and listening to

Kathy's labored breathing and her spells of painful coughing. Lloyd must be mistaken, she decided finally. He'd probably gotten more shaken up than she'd realized. Why on earth would Uncle Lester, of all people, deliberately force the pickup truck off the road? Unless he had done something . . . Meg drifted off into a troubled sleep, dreams of measles and wrecks on dark roads all jumbled together.

When she opened her eyes again, the portholes were gray and everything was hushed on board the *Tessie*. No sound came from the other cabins or Kathy's bunk. No sound at all. Fear caught at Meg's heart. Was it possible that Kathy . . . ? She raised herself slowly from her bunk, got up, and leaned over Kathy. Her face was pale and extraordinarily peaceful. Meg laid her cheek close to Kathy's. It felt cool, so cool that for a heartbreaking moment Meg thought she was dead. Then she felt a slight movement of air. Kathy was breathing. Meg touched her forehead and found it damp with perspiration. The fever had broken, and Kathy was deep in natural sleep.

16

LLOYD SLEPT LATE the next day. After breakfast Meg slipped into the fo'c'sle and sat on Jamie's bunk drinking a second cup of tea. Lloyd stirred and turned over, groping for his glasses. Meg handed them to him. He sat up. "What time is it?"

" 'Bout nine-thirty. You up t'telling me what happened last night?"

"Guess so." Lloyd took a sip of Meg's tea. "We were drivin' down that lonely stretch of road on Meekins Neck.

We were almost to Honga when we saw this car ahead parked with its headlights blazin'. Dad slowed down 'cause he thought someone might need help. He pulled alongside. Then all of a sudden, he pushed the accelerator to the floor and tore off."

"Why'd he do that?"

"He'd seen their guns. They were poachers headlightin' for deer." Meg looked at him quizzically. "The idea is to shine lights into the woods at night, lurin' the deer out into the open, where it's easy to shoot them. Headlightin's illegal any time, and now it's not even huntin' season!"

"But why'd you get forced off the road?"

Lloyd sighed. He was tired of explaining. "Because those men were breakin' the law. Don't you see? I don't think they really meant to hurt us. Just scare us some and hinder our gettin' to the police before they could get away. Their license plate was smeared with mud. On purpose, I guess. What they didn't count on was our recognizing the car."

"And it was Uncle Lester's car?"

"Sure was!"

"D'you think Dad'll do anything about it?"

Lloyd lowered his eyes and drew a circle on the sheets with his finger. "Don't think so . . . 'cause of Aunt Lavinia."

That afternoon Lloyd had to repeat his story for Captain Noah's benefit. His father was still in no condition to talk to anyone. The pickup truck had been damaged in the wreck, and since it belonged to Captain Noah, he wanted to know how it had happened. As he listened to Lloyd's story, his face darkened into a scowl.

Next day Captain Noah drove to Cambridge and confronted Lester Messick with Lloyd's story. Lester listened condescendingly, then flatly denied any knowledge of the accident.

"I was home with Lavinia that evening, Captain. You can ask her if you like."

"That's not what Lloyd says. He says it was your car."

Uncle Lester shook his head. "Well, it's too bad the lad says such things! I guess it's my word against his. You'll not get anyone else to come forward."

"We'll see about that!" Captain Noah growled and stormed out of the office.

The last Wednesday in August was Kathy's birthday, her third. Meg wanted to bake her a cake. Kathy had made a good recovery from the measles, and when Meg found her, she was admiring a doll's bonnet she'd just tied on Scaredy's head. "Let's ask Mrs. Whitelock if we can use her oven. I'll bet she doesn't even know it's your birthday. No. Leave Scaredy here. I don't know where old Skipper is."

Obediently Kathy put Scaredy down and was soon skipping along the path that led to the gate in the picket fence.

"Come in," Mrs. Whitelock called when Meg tapped on the screen door.

She was sitting on one of her stiff-backed Victorian chairs, face flushed and hair awry. Her left leg rested on a stool. "Kathy, you're a pleasin' sight for old eyes!" she said. "You all better now?"

"Uh-huh. All better, and it's my birthday!"

"Dear, dear! Think of that! If this knee of mine wasn't pesterin' me, I'd bake you a cake."

Meg said, "I've a cake mix, eggs, and milk. All we need is an oven."

Mrs. Whitelock chuckled. "Aren't you the one, Meg Evans! Well, go along, get your stuff and come on back. You can use my oven and welcome. I'll be with you in a minute, soon as I finish that window."

Meg looked at the fan of glass above the front door. A stepladder stood beside it. She saw a bottle of window cleaner in the old lady's hand. "Mrs. Whitelock! Were you thinking of washing the glass above the door?"

"Well . . . I had a mind to. That fan's so pretty when it's clean and shiny! But the ladder wobbles, and my knee wobbles. It's—"

"Here! Give me that bottle. You shouldn't be climbing around on ladders!"

Meg climbed nimbly to the top of the stepladder, sprayed the glass in the handsome old fan, polished it, and was down again within three minutes.

"That looks grand!" Mrs. Whitelock beamed. "Y'know this house is gettin' t'be almost too much. Help from Honga's undependable and comes dear. The captain and I often talk about what we should do, 'specially since my knee started actin' up. Sometimes we think we should sell and move to Florida. But I'd sure hate to leave the old place! Been here forty-two years."

"Oh, Mrs. Whitelock! Don't think of leavin'!" Meg begged. "I couldn't bear to have anyone else livin' in this house! And the boatyard . . . why, it'd be a disaster without you and Cap'n Noah!"

Mrs. Whitelock took off her glasses and touched her apron to her eyes. Without her glasses, her brown eyes were wonderfully soft and warm. "Well, that's nice to hear! There's not a better feelin' in this world than knowin' you're wanted." She rose carefully from her chair, favoring her knee. "Come along then, girls. Let's bake that cake. I'll set the oven."

"Can I please play in your attic, Gramma Bessie?" Kathy asked.

"Sure can, dearie! It's warm up there, but I guess at your age you'll not mind."

Kathy ran up the stairs.

"It's nice havin' Kathy around," Mrs. Whitelock continued, on her way to the kitchen. "She's well mannered and good company besides."

With the cake in the oven and Kathy occupied, Meg went back to the *Tessie* to make a sandwich for her dad. She was worried about him. He was working too hard on the *Wind Mistress*. He hardly stopped long enough to eat. The sloop was promised for the Labor Day races, and she was still on the ways. He was not one to go back on a contract.

With his sandwich in her hand Meg stood watching her father and two workmen step the mast. They tipped the mast's end into the hole in the sloop's deck. It slipped through well enough and stood tall and steady. The men stepped back with satisfaction. Meg breathed easier.

"Super, Dad!" she called. "Can you take time off t'eat now? I brought you a sandwich."

The other men had gone for their lunch boxes, but Mr. Evans lingered to check the rake of the mast. Then, with toolbox in hand, he started below to drive home the chocks.

"Dad!" Meg called again. "I brought you a sandwich. How 'bout stopping your work long enough t'eat?"

Her father peered down at her. "Aye, I could eat now. You bring me somethin'?"

"A sandwich, Dad." Meg shook her head, puzzled. Ever since the accident her father had seemed preoccupied. Sure, he had the *Wind Mistress* on his mind, the deadline he was up against. But there was something else bothering him, Meg felt certain. Once she overheard him talking to himself . . . something about not stirrin' up a pot o' trouble.

Suddenly, Meg remembered the cake. "I'll leave the sandwich here, Dad. Gotta go! There's a cake in Mrs. Whitelock's oven."

The next day Lloyd found a sea gull with a broken wing. He and Jamie had gone fishing soon after lunch in an old rowboat belonging to Captain Noah. They anchored off Barren Island and dropped their lines overboard. An hour passed, but nothing so much as nibbled on their hooks. Jamie pulled his line in and looked with disgust at the tired gray worm dangling from his hook. Then his face brightened. "Let's explore Barren Island! We've never done that. Maybe there's treasure! What we want t'do is look for a landmark, something special like an extra tall tree."

They beached the rowboat and started walking along the sand. The island was long and narrow, a strip of scrub and sandy soil with a low marshy place in its middle. They spotted nothing like a landmark that would attract a pirate's eye, but when they pushed through some beach plum on the windward side, Lloyd saw the sea gull. He lay on the sand almost in the water, one wing stretched out. At first the boys thought he was dead, but when Lloyd touched him, he lifted his head, opened glazed eyes, and hopped a few feet up the beach dragging his wing. The boys followed cautiously, trying not to frighten him

more. When he lay still again, exhausted, they bent over him.

"Wow! He's big!" Jamie said in an awed voice. "He looks so much bigger this way than they do flyin'."

"What happened to you, poor old gull?" Lloyd said. He hated to see wild things in distress.

"Maybe a storm blew him against somethin' hard, a cliff or the glass in one of the lighthouses. He could've floated here."

"There've been no storms that I heard of. At any rate, he'll starve if we leave him here. Jamie, let's take him back to the *Tessie*. I think I could make a splint for his wing. Meg will help."

The sea gull struggled when Lloyd pounced. But Lloyd held on and finally got the big bird securely tucked under one arm. He stroked the smooth feathers on the gull's back with his other hand. After a while the gull grew quiet. Jamie shoved the boat into the water, and they climbed in.

When the boys showed Meg the gull she shook her head. Tending wild birds was discouraging business, but she was unable to resist the pleading in Lloyd's eyes. She tore an old dish towel into narrow strips for him to use in binding the wing. He'd already found a splinter of wood, strong but light, to use as a splint. "D'you think you can hold him, Meg?"

"I'll try."

"I'll help you," Jamie said.

It was all Meg and Jamie together could do to keep the gull quiet while Lloyd tried to set his wing. The gull fought them hard, flapping his uninjured wing and pecking at their hands and arms. He was strong in spite of his injury.

"I'm afraid I'm hurting him," Lloyd said, "but it can't be helped. I've got to get those bones in line."

"He's scared, too," Meg said. "Scared frantic, poor thing!"

Kathy watched with interest from a safe distance. "Poor birdie!" she murmured from time to time.

"Let's call him Cecil," Jamie said. "Cecil the sea gull."

"Okay," Lloyd agreed. "That's as good a name as any. There. The bones feel straight. Hold tight a minute more while I bind it."

"Where d'you boys plan to keep him?" Meg asked. "A fox or raccoon's sure to get him if you leave him flopping helpless around the shore!"

"We could put him in a crab trap," Jamie volunteered. "There's an old one lying on the other side of the boat-house. We could put it up in the *Tessie*'s bow out of the way. Scaredy wouldn't bother him there."

Lloyd split the end of the last strip of dish towel so that he could tie it securely around splint and wing to hold the entire affair together. "Okay, let's get it. Can you keep Cecil still till we get back, Meg? If he flops around a lot, he may break the splint."

"Well, hurry!"

As the boys slid down the boarding ladder, Lloyd noticed something peculiar. Water from the Bay reached almost to the ladder. He'd never seen so high a tide!

That evening he asked his father about it. "What does it mean, the tide comin' in like that?"

The family had brought their supper up on deck be-cause it was too hot to eat in the cabin. Mr. Evans leaned back against the mast. "Hard t'say for sure," he said. "Some weather makin' up in the lower Bay, I reckon. Somethin' local. By the way, tomorrow early we'll take the *Wind Mistress* across to Solomons. We'll be wantin' two o' you kids t'come along t'handle sail."

"Why can't we all go?" Meg asked. "Kathy could wear a life preserver."

Her father looked at her in surprise. "Why? Why because a yacht under sail's no place for a three-year-old. Besides, there wouldn't be room comin' back. That old waterman friend of the cap'n's, Galen Godbey, is bringin' us back in his motor launch. It's only fit for five." He took a coin out of his pocket. "Jamie'll have to go; I'll not leave him here alone with Kathy. Call it, Meg."

"Heads." She lost the toss.

Lloyd looked almost guilty. "Look, Meg, if you really want to—I mean sure, I'd like t'go, but fair's fair, and you've done a lot of babysittin' lately. I could look after Kathy all right."

Meg almost accepted his offer. Then she changed her mind. Fair *was* fair. She had lost the toss. "Nope. I'll go another time." She gathered up the dirty plates and went below. But she was grateful to Lloyd.

Lloyd walked to the bow to see how Cecil the sea gull was getting on. He found him sitting forlornly on one corner of the crab trap, his splinted wing extending stiffly from his body at an awkward angle. He hadn't touched the bit of fish they'd put there for him or drunk any of the water. Lloyd turned away and looked over the side of the ship at the sun, as it set in a scarlet haze. Not a breath of air was stirring.

17

THE WEATHER lost little of its heat overnight. It was warm and sticky in the fo'c'sle when Lloyd woke up. Hearing voices on deck, he boosted himself through the hatch. Meg was talking to Captain Noah.

"Dad's gone to the showers," she said. "Can I give him a message?"

"Thanks, honey. I'll wait. Mornin', Lloyd!"

"Hi, Cap'n Noah!"

"You ready to cross the Bay?"

"Sure. When d'we start?"

"The sooner, the better! There's a storm brewin'."

Mr. Evans appeared at the bottom of the boarding ladder with a towel flung over his shoulder. Captain Noah leaned over the rail. "Tyler, they're broadcastin' storm warnin's, one of those tropical disturbances come up from the Caribbean. They're callin' her Agatha. She hit Hatteras durin' the night. Did a heap of damage! Winds up t'seventy mile an hour and wicked high tides! No question, she's comin' our way."

Mr. Evans looked out over the Bay at the clear sky and glassy blue water. "What d'you reckon we should do?"

"Likely we'll be all right if we start right away. These summer storms don't travel real fast. I sure hate not deliverin' a boat on schedule."

"The boys and I can leave anytime."

"Good. But before we go, I'd like t'move the *Nellie Byrd* and the *J. P. Leonard* up near the bridge in Honga. There's more protection there just in case it should start t'blow and us not be around. Give me a hand movin' them; then we'll shove off."

"I'll fix sandwiches," Meg said.

"Good girl. My Bessie's packin' a basket with fruit and such."

Lloyd dropped down into the fo'c'sle and shook Jamie. "Hey, wake up! We'll be goin' soon."

Jamie sat up, stretched, and yawned. "I'm ready," he said, running his hand through his tousled hair. He swung his legs over the edge of the bunk. He yawned again prodigiously, then picked his jeans off the floor and pulled them on over the underwear he'd slept in.

Meg, Kathy, and Mrs. Whitelock walked out to the

end of the main dock to wave the sailors off. Old Skipper stood beside them, wagging his tail and whining, his way of asking to be taken along. Captain Noah scratched the dog's ears. "Next time, old boy," he said. "There'd not be room in the launch comin' back." He settled himself at the *Wind Mistress*'s helm and started her auxiliary engine. It coughed, sputtered, and died. He tried again, and it caught hold.

Lloyd and Jamie lifted the lines off the dock's pilings, threw them on deck, and jumped aboard. The yacht moved slowly away from the dock.

"Bring a present, Daddy!" Kathy called after them.

"Well, now, Kathy, don't know about that." Her father's mouth twitched at the corners. "We're just goin' 'cross the Bay, not t'foreign lands! You be a good girl and mind Meg."

"Don't do anything reckless, Noah!" Mrs. Whitelock called.

"You know me better'n that, Bessie! See you girls behave!"

The *Wind Mistress*'s small propeller pushed her along the narrow channel that led across Tar Bay to the Chesapeake. From shore Meg noticed that the engine was skipping. It worried her. The *Wind Mistress* might need her auxiliary if the storm caught her.

When the *Wind Mistress* was well away from the dock, the group on shore started slowly back toward the boatyard. Skipper followed, his head hanging and his tail between his legs. Meg felt sort of dejected herself. She would have liked to go along, too.

"Think I'll close the house against the heat," Mrs. Whitelock said. "Pull the blinds where the sun shines in.

Hot as it is, it's hard t'believe summer's most over. Say, why don't you girls come have lunch with me? I've lemonade and plenty of stuff for sandwiches."

"We'd like that," Meg said. "Mrs. Whitelock, did you ever wish you could do the things the captain did, instead of stayin' home and tendin' the house?"

"Don't know as I ever thought about it, dearie. I always took it for granted that the house was mine t'look after and the boatyard his. I know, though, that young women are lookin' at things different today. Come over 'round noontime. I'll be glad t'have some company."

Before going to lunch, Meg visited the mailbox. In it she found a note and a check from Mr. Pruitt on Smith Island. He'd sold one of her sketches. At first, she could hardly believe her eyes. When she'd made sure everything about the note and check was genuine, she picked Kathy up and danced around the mailbox in delight. Then she hustled Kathy over to Mrs. Whitelock's to tell her the good news.

"That's real fine, Meg," Mrs. Whitelock said, giving her a little pat on the back. "You're an honest t'goodness artist now!"

It was too hot to stay on the *Tessie* that afternoon, so Meg and Kathy put on their swimming suits. Kathy stayed on the small strip of sand by the main dock, but Meg ran out to the end and dived in. The water felt marvelously cool and refreshing. She surfaced feeling that it wasn't such a bad day after all. The check from Smith Island had made all the difference.

Kathy was having a fine time filling a muffin tin with muddy sand and turning the muffins out on a board to bake in the sun. When Meg had enough of swimming, she stretched out gingerly on the hot dock, letting the water from her dripping body gradually cool the boards. She lay there daydreaming . . . She was at the opening of her own art show, held in a large gallery. It might be New York, or more likely Baltimore. Her pictures were beautifully framed, artistically displayed. "Lovely work," people were saying. In another scene, she and Peter Dawson were aboard a ship not unlike the *Tessie C. Price*, sailing with a fresh breeze into a sunset sky over the broad reaches of the Chesapeake.

"Meggie?"

"Huh?"

Kathy was patting her on the back with sandy fingers. "Tired of muffins," she said. Her eyes were heavy.

Meg settled Kathy on her bunk for a nap, then took her sketching pad out on deck. She wanted to draw a profile of Cecil the sea gull. She'd never before had a chance to study the head of a bird up close. A sudden puff of wind of surprising vigor snatched a piece of paper off the deck and sent it sailing into the big oak tree next door.

Time sped by. The sketch wouldn't come out right. When Kathy came stumbling up the companionway rubbing sleep from her eyes, Meg was glad to put her pad and pencil aside.

"Let's walk out to the end of the dock," she said, "and see if we can see Daddy comin' back. It's about time if all went well."

The boatyard was stewing in the shimmering heat. It was an effort even to move. Kathy dragged her feet as they walked out onto the dock. Meg strained her eyes searching for a black speck that could be Mr. Godbey's motor launch, but there was nothing to be seen except gulls flying low and a far distant freighter headed north. Suddenly, the sun was caught by a huge cloud bank, and the Bay took on a threatening look. With the darkening sky came gusts of moisture-laden wind seeming to blow from all directions at once. They tumbled the hair about Meg's face. Feeling uneasy about her father and the boys, Meg started back. Kathy reached up for her hand.

The tide that had been extraordinarily high that morning was now correspondingly low. Walking toward the shore, Meg saw that seaweed normally under water lay flat on the mud and sand. At the foot of the dock an old tire she never suspected of being there lay partly exposed with strings of bright green algae clinging to it like an exotic fringe.

Back on the *Tessie's* deck Meg folded two deck chairs and put them below. They were followed by several pillows, towels, a magazine or two, and her sketching materials. Then she hauled down the flag.

"What you do?" Kathy asked.

"I'm making ready for Agatha. It looks as though she'll be here before long, and I don't think she's a nice lady."

"Who Agatha?"

"Agatha's a storm. She'll bring rain and wind."

In the bow Cecil fluttered anxiously in his crab trap. Meg wondered what to do about him. If she released him, he'd be certain to do further damage to his wing. If she left him where he was, he'd be half drowned by the downpour that was surely coming. She decided the best thing would be to put him in the fo'c'sle. With some difficulty, caused partly by Kathy trying to help, she managed to move the crab trap over to the forward hatch and tip it down through the opening. Going below, she pulled it through and made it level across the two bunks. Then she went on deck again and closed the forward hatch, fastening the hooks that held the cover securely to the deck.

In the cabin, wind made the small curtains stand out straight and stiff from the portholes. All day it had been stuffy below. Now the cabin was drafty as a shed. Meg screwed the portholes shut.

Kathy had picked Scaredy up and was wandering aimlessly about, holding her tight around the middle, legs dangling down. Finally the kitten twisted loose and hid under Jamie's bunk. The sight of the cat excited Cecil, who set up a squawking. Meg dragged Scaredy out of the fo'c'sle and closed the door.

"Meggie, let's go to Grandma Bessie's," Kathy said.

Meg was listening to the wind sounds, a sighing in the branches of the trees and a singing in the rigging that began as a low moan and grew more and more shrill before it ceased altogether. "All right," she agreed. She rather welcomed the idea of sharing her uneasiness with someone older than Kathy.

They climbed out on deck and found the branches of the trees in the Whitelock's yard doing a frenzied wind dance. The tide was coming in fast. It was already deep under the *Tessie's* bowsprit. The wind on their backs nudged them toward the boarding ladder. But just as they reached it, it began to pour.

"We'd be drenched if we went to Grandma Bessie's now, lollipop," Meg said. "We'll go later when the rain's stopped. Get back inside. I'll fix some supper for us."

Kathy scrambled back down the companionway. As Meg followed, distant thunder sounded like the roll of many drums. Meg pulled the hatch cover over their heads and closed and bolted the small folding door that sealed the cabin tight against bad weather. A burst of lightning shivered and quivered around the *Tessie*, making the portholes into circles of light. When they were snuffed out, it seemed almost dark in the cabin. Meg lit the kerosene lamps to combat the gloom.

The storm grew rapidly more violent. It would abate a little, then reach peaks of ever greater fury. With shaky hands Meg put together some supper. The girls ate without talking, listening instead to all the unfamiliar sounds—the rushing wind, the thunder's roar, the creaking of the *Tessie*'s old timbers. The rain blowing against her hull sounded like buckets of water dashed one after the other against her side by some giant of the storm. Lightning struck nearby, and the portholes glared like beasts' eyes. The flash was followed by a sharp crack of thunder that sent Kathy into Meg's arms crying with terror.

Meg held her close. "It's all right, lollipop. Agatha's a bad girl, but she can't hurt us, really. We're snug and safe here in the *Tessie*."

"She scares my ears!"

"She'll grow tired after a while and go away. Let's put your 'jamies on and have a story."

"Daddy come?"

"Yes, Daddy'll come. But it may be late—after you're asleep. They'll have to drive, and it's a long way 'round."

After the story Kathy obediently turned on her side, held her special blanket under her chin, and closed her eyes.

Meg returned to the main cabin, where she went again to a porthole. It was black outside, but she could hear limbs snapping and crashing to the ground. She wished she'd taken Kathy to Whitelock's earlier in the afternoon. Now it would be too dangerous. She took out her sewing basket intending to sew a patch on Jamie's jeans. The *Tessie* shuddered in the wind's grasp. Meg looked up to see trickles of water finding their way inside the cabin.

They made dark squiggles on the woodwork. Meg pushed the basket aside. Her fingers were trembling too much for sewing. She sat with her hands folded tightly in her lap.

Suddenly she heard a tremendous crash, much louder than any before. She rushed to a porthole and saw by the lightning that the Whitelock's huge old oak had toppled. The tree covered most of the lawn. Some of its small branches lay on the roof of the house. At the same time she caught glints of light on water stretching away from the *Tessie*. She ran to the other side to look out. It was dark again. She waited. When the lightning came, it shone on water almost up to the porch of the store. The *Tessie* was surrounded. She might have been sitting in the middle of a lake.

The noise of the tree crashing had awakened Kathy, who lay wailing with fright. The *Tessie*'s hull was swaying gently as Meg started toward her. She steadied herself with her hands. She reached Kathy's bunk, sank down beside her, and put her arms around her. The wind grew stronger still. In a passion of wailing, howling, and screeching it rained blows like those of a sledgehammer on the *Tessie*'s transom. With a groan of protesting timbers, the *Tessie* started to slip forward. Meg could feel the old boat as she slid, scraped, and bumped over mud and sand. At first she moved by inches. Then she gathered speed, and the scraping and bumping became more violent. Suddenly it ceased altogether, and Meg knew the ship was floating free. The *Tessie* was being blown out onto Tar Bay.

Clutching Kathy, Meg closed her eyes and braced herself for the moment when the creaky old hull would fall apart and dump them into the water. She felt waves under the keel. The *Tessie* rose to meet them. But when she fell shuddering into the troughs between, Meg thought each time would be the last . . . and most likely the last of her and Kathy. Though she was a strong swimmer, there would be little chance for them on a wild night like this. Help us, dear God! she prayed. Please help us!

The girls remained clutched in each other's arms for some time. Then, quite suddenly, Agatha seemed to have worn herself out. The *Tessie* rose and fell more gently, the sound of the wind died to a whimper, and the rain ceased its pounding on the cabin roof. Meg opened her eyes. Through the porthole above Kathy's head she caught a fleeting glimpse of the moon. She let go of Kathy and raised herself on the bunk to look out. "Kathy! Kathy!" she cried. "Agatha's gone away! We're going to be all right!" She laughed shakily. "We're going for a boat ride, Kathy, that's all—a moonlight sail on Tar Bay!"

She stepped down to take a look from the other side, and her moment of elation left her. She'd stepped into water up to her ankles. The *Tessie* hadn't fallen apart all at once, but she was going down all the same. She was rapidly sinking.

Meg climbed back onto Kathy's bunk and tried to think calmly about how they might save themselves. Tar Bay was notoriously shallow. On a normal sort of night, even if the *Tessie* sank, she wouldn't have far to go. The cabin roof would likely remain out of water after she'd settled on the bottom. They could perch there all night if necessary, wet and uncomfortable but safe. But this night was different. The water was so high that when the *Tessie* sank, there might be something left to cling to . . . and there might not! Besides, there was the chilling possibility she might stay afloat just long enough to be swept out on-to the Chesapeake and then sink! One thing was clear to

Meg. They must get out of the cabin before it filled with water.

"Kathy," she said, "We're goin' up on deck."

"In the dark?"

"The dark won't hurt us. Maybe we'll take a little swim, then spend the night at Grandma Bessie's."

This prospect suited Kathy. She started to slide off her bunk but drew back when her feet touched the water. "Water's inside."

"Never mind. We'll just splash right through. Here. I'll carry you."

With Kathy in her arms, Meg sloshed through the cabin. She put Kathy on the companionway ladder, then stood beside her to open the hatch. She shoved back the bolt on the little folding door and pushed on it. Nothing happened. Using both hands she pushed again, pushed with all her strength. The door refused to budge. Swollen with rain water and hammered into its frame by the wind, it was stuck fast.

She thought of the hatch cover in the fo'c'sle which could be opened by pushing up, only to remember the care with which she'd bolted it down on the outside. She tried to slide the hatch cover over their heads back without opening the door. It was impossible. All she did was break several fingernails. Again she attacked the door, pounding on it with her fists. She paused for breath and, looking down, saw that the water in the cabin had reached their step. What if they were trapped? She had a sickening vision of their drowning with their heads bobbing against the cabin's roof. In a frenzy she pounded on the door once more until her fists were bruised and raw.

"Open up!" she screamed. "Open up, you stupid little door! Let us out!"

Frightened by Meg's screaming, Kathy began to wail. The sound sobered Meg. She slumped down and put her arms around Kathy. Kathy stopped her noise, and they both sat very still, numb with fear. Suddenly, Meg saw Aunt Lavinia's face before her, wearing her usual patronizing look. She seemed to be saying, as she'd said so often— You're too young to look after a small child. In a fix you'd go all to pieces. You'd have no idea what t'do!

Meg straightened up and looked around the cabin. What she needed was something heavy to use as a battering ram. Her eyes fell on the little red fire extinguisher Captain Noah had hung by the stove. "Hold tight, Kathy," she said. "I'll be right back."

She plunged through waist-deep water to reach the stove and jerked the fire extinguisher from the wall. She was glad of the weight of it in her hands as she floundered back to the companionway. She planted her feet firmly and braced her back against the steps. Then she aimed the red cylinder at the hinge of the door and hurled it forward as hard as she could. There was a splintering sound, the door popped out, and the fire extinguisher skittered across the deck.

Meg took a deep breath of the air that poured in from outside, giddy with relief. "Out you go," she said to Kathy, giving her a boost. "Hold tight to the rail, lollipop!"

All manner of things were now floating around the cabin–the bunk cushions, her wooden salad bowl, the cutting board. She heard a meow and saw Scaredy clinging to the curtain rod above a porthole. Meg set her outside on the cabin roof. Water had filled the forward cabins. It was too bad about Cecil, but there was nothing Meg could do for him. In the main cabin the kerosene lamps flickered and went out. Meg captured a floating bunk cushion, pushed it ahead of her through the hatch, and climbed onto the deck.

Kathy was holding onto the rail as she'd been told to do. Meg stood beside her for a moment to get her bearings. The moon was playing hide and seek in the clouds. When at last it showed its face, she could see the boatyard clearly. She'd have a long swim before it was shallow enough to wade. But the deck was already awash. The *Tessie*, though sinking, was still drifting toward the Chesapeake. There was no time to lose.

She placed the bunk cushion on the other side of the *Tessie*'s rail and put Kathy in the center of it. She was glad to see the cushion bore Kathy's weight. "Now stay flat on your tummy, Kathy, and hold on with both hands. Don't let go no matter what! I'm goin' to tow you t'shore. Don't let go! D'you understand?"

Kathy's eyes were wide, but she nodded her head.

Meg kicked off her sneakers. Then, still holding onto Kathy's raft, she slipped over the rail. With a hard push of her legs against the *Tessie*'s hull, she began swimming. She held the raft with one hand and sidestroked toward the shore with the other arm. The cushion was heavy and awkward to pull. She was soon tired. She rested a minute, treading water and clinging to Kathy's raft. Then she took another dozen strokes, and another. She rested again. Her legs felt the pull of the tide, which was working against her. She must keep going or lose way. "You all right, Kathy?"

Kathy nodded her head.

Meg began swimming again. For a long time she thought only of making her arms and legs do what she told them, stroke, legs apart, kick, stroke, over and over again. Her muscles ached, her heart was pounding, and she sucked air in painful gasps. The cushion raft was growing heavier. Now water-logged, it rode lower in the water. She wondered if they'd make it, if she had the strength to take one more stroke. Then she heard a dog bark. She raised her head from the water and saw a light. The shore was closer than she'd dared to hope. She felt for the bottom with her toes. Nothing. She swam ten more strokes and tried again. This time her toes felt mud. "Help!" she cried. "We're out here in the water. Help us, please!"

The light swept slowly around, coming toward them. "Is that you, Meg?" a woman's voice called.

"Yes, yes! Kathy and me!" Meg answered.

The beam of Mrs. Whitelock's flashlight found them at last, making a bright path to the shore. Meg waded along it pulling the raft. When the water was below her knees, she picked Kathy up and carried her. Mrs. Whitelock waded toward them, not caring for the wetting she was getting, and soon was hugging them hard. "Thank God you're safe!" she cried.

"Mrs. Whitelock!" Meg said. "Your light and Skipper's bark . . . To think you'd come lookin' for us with your bad knee and all!"

"Well, I had t'do somethin'! Soon after the oak crashed, I saw from my window the *Tessie*'d gone out. I tried to call the Coast Guard, but the phone was dead. I don't trust myself drivin' that truck, 'specially on a night like this un's been! I didn't rightly know what t'do. But I couldn't sit in my house twiddlin', so I came lookin' for you. I was scared you'd gone down . . . scared half t'death!"

"We had some bad moments, Kathy and me. Aunt Lavinia helped."

"Aunt Lavinia? Whatever are you talkin' about?"

"Never mind, Mrs. Whitelock, dear. It's hard to explain."

With Mrs. Whitelock's arm around her waist and Skipper dancing about and barking with surprising vigor for so old a dog, Meg sloshed through mud and water to the porch of the store, where she put Kathy down. Her arms felt crampy, and she was shivering all over.

"The temperature's taken a big drop!" Mrs. Whitelock said. "September's in the air. Soon's you've caught your breath, we'll head for the house."

"Me good girl!" Kathy said in a firm voice. "Held on tight."

"Yes, you did," Meg said. "We'd never've made it otherwise!"

All at once the moon sailed out into a large clear place in the night sky, making a broad path all the way across Tar Bay. In the light, almost to Barren Island, Meg saw two whitish spars, all that remained above water of the *Tessie C. Price.*

18

MEG OPENED her eyes. Bright sunlight dappled the walls, and a breeze billowed the sheer curtains at a window. For a moment she couldn't remember where she was. Then the events of the night before came rushing back, and she knew she and Kathy were in Mrs. Whitelock's spare bedroom lying on her old-fashioned mahogany bed. Its four spiral posts rose grandly above her head. She was wearing one of Mrs. Whitelock's nightgowns.

She slipped out of bed and saw her clothes lying in a damp heap on the floor near Kathy's wet pajamas. In need

197

of something to wear, she opened the door to the closet. The only thing she could find that would serve her purpose was a pink ruffled dress with several buttons missing. She put it on, making a big fold in the front and tying the sash tight to hold it in place. The breeze slammed the closet door, and Kathy sat up in bed. She was wearing a pajama top of Captain Noah's, the sleeves rolled up and the neck pinned with a large safety pin. She looked at Meg and giggled. "Funny dress!"

"Yes, it's funny. But you know where *our* clothes are! I'm goin' t'fix breakfast. What would you like?"

"Sugarpops."

"I'll see if Grandma Bessie has some."

In the kitchen she laid the table for breakfast. Kathy had tagged along behind. Meg pulled a high stool over to the table and settled her on it with her cereal. Then she heated water for coffee and poached eggs.

"Mornin', girls!" Mrs. Whitelock said from the doorway. "That coffee sure smells good!" Old Skipper followed at her heels and lay down by the table.

"Would you like a poached egg and some bacon?" Meg asked.

" 'Deed I would, dearie!" She seated herself at the table across from Kathy. "It's nice being waited on after years of doin' for myself."

Meg brought the coffeepot to the table. "Mrs. White-lock, are you worrried about the others?"

"I'll be relieved t'hear from them, that's a fact. But I'm not goin' t'commence t'worry just yet. Galen's a cautious sort. He'd not take to the Bay in a small boat when a storm's brewin'." Her eyes began to twinkle. "See you found somethin' t'wear. Must say our shapes are some different! I'll find somethin' else for you and Kathy after breakfast. I think my girls may have left a dress or two behind."

Meg poached the eggs, fixed toast and bacon, and set Mrs. Whitelock's plate before her. She fixed a plate for herself and sat down. But she didn't eat any of the food, only broke her toast into smaller and smaller pieces. "Mrs. Whitelock, can I talk to you about something? I have an idea. Maybe it's no good, and you can tell me so. But I'd like, at least, to tell you—"

Mrs. Whitelock looked at Meg over the rim of her coffee mug. "Go ahead, dear. Never hurts t'talk things over."

"We've got some problems now and . . . well, I think you do, too. Could we maybe help each other out?"

"Helpin' each other is what good livin's all about, Meg. What d'you have in mind?"

"We'll need a place t'live now the *Tessie*'s gone down. Then there's Kathy. A plan has t'be made for her after I go back to school. I was wondering—"

"You were wondering if you could stay with me and the Captain for a while. Of course you can! That way we'll settle two problems at once. You can help me some around the house, and I can keep an eye on Kathy." Beaming, she put down her coffee mug and folded her hands in her lap.

Meg jumped up from the table and hugged her. "Mrs. Whitelock, I could . . . I could just hug you to pieces! You just solved everything!"

Still smiling, Mrs. Whitelock patted down her hair, which had been rumpled by Meg's exuberance. Then she said seriously. "No, Meg, it's not my doin'. A large part of the solvin' was yours. You've proved t'anyone has eyes t'see the good sense that lies behind those gray eyes of yours and the abidin' affection you hold in your heart."

Meg turned away, her eyes made misty by praise. She slowly returned to her side of the table. When she was seated, Mrs. Whitelock leaned toward her. "Meg, there's just one thing. Let's the two of us keep this to ourselves till I have a chance t'talk it over with the Captain. Agreed?"

"D'you think he'll—"

Skipper barked once, twice, then walked stiff-legged to the door. They heard a car turn into the boatyard.

"They're here!" Meg ran out the kitchen door in time to see Jamie piling out of the back of the car stopped in the driveway. Meg headed through the gate in the picket fence straight into her father's arms.

"I was worried 'bout you, Meg," he said, holding her. "Real worried! Where's Kathy?"

"In the kitchen with Mrs. Whitelock."

"Where's the *Tessie*?" Lloyd asked, staring at the place she'd been.

"Out there!" Meg pointed.

Everyone looked across Tar Bay and saw the *Tessie's* masts and her deck now visible but awash.

"Wow!" Jamie ran as close to the water as he could, calling back over his shoulder, "Where were you when she went out?"

"On board, Kathy and I."

At that moment Mrs. Whitelock and Kathy appeared from the house. Seeing her father, Kathy ran to him. He swung her off the ground.

"Hi, Daddy! Me good girl! Held on tight!"

"She did that!" Meg said and told them how she and Kathy had abandoned the *Tessie*. The men were silent for a minute after she'd finished. Then her father said.

"You did right t'get off her while you could. Thank the Lord you made it! Looks like we'll have t'find another place t'live."

Captain Noah's eyes were traveling over the boatyard. It was a mess. The roof had been half torn off the store, the smaller of the two docks was gone, and fallen branches were strewn all about. The receding water had left an ugly layer of muck over everything.

"The white oak's fallen, toppled by the wind," Mrs. Whitelock said. "It was a wild night, Noah!"

"We had a wild crossin'! Lost a sail to the wind, and our auxiliary quit on us. A time or two, I didn't think we'd make it! Drivin' 'round the Bay in the storm was no picnic either, as Galen can testify."

"Well, let's go sit in the kitchen where we can be more comfortable. Galen, won't you join us? You look like you could use some coffee."

"Thanks a lot, ma'am, but I'll be headin' back. There'll be plenty that needs tendin' to 'round Solomon's!" He climbed into his car.

"Many thanks for seein' us safely home," Captain Noah said.

"We're much obliged," Mr. Evans added. "Me and my boys."

"Don't mention it. I'm just glad we found your families safe." Mr. Godbey started his engine and headed out the drive.

Jamie rejoined them as they walked toward the house. "Hey, Meg, that's some dress you're wearin'!"

"Glad you like it! My own clothes are damp . . . naturally."

In the kitchen Mrs. Whitelock began scrambling eggs for the men. Meg laid more slices of bacon in the skillet to fry. The men settled themselves at the table, the boys sat on the floor, and Kathy climbed onto her father's knee. Mrs. Whitelock poured coffee.

"The bridge over the Blackwater was out," Captain Noah said, holding his coffee mug in both hands. "This mornin' we had t'wait till they made temporary repairs. The water went down pretty good durin' the night, but there's lots of damage on Meekins Neck!" He took a large swallow of coffee.

Jamie wrinkled his nose. "Bacon's burnin', Meg!"

Meg looked at the skillet and made a wry face. "Wish no one would talk about anything interestin' till I finish cooking!"

Captain Noah's eyes twinkled. "Well now, honey, there's not a lot t'talk 'bout this mornin' that isn't interestin'! What about the *Tessie*, Tyler? D'you want t'try and save her?"

"I'd like t'take a closer look. We raised her once. Mebbe we can do it again."

"Well, let's drive over to the bridge and see if the *Nellie Byrd* and the *Leonard* took any damage. If the *Leonard*'s in workin' order, we can take her out to the *Tessie*."

"I'd be obliged, Noah. Sooner we get our gear off the *Tessie*, the better! The tide's goin' out pretty good now. We should get t'her before it turns."

"You boys want t'come?" the captain asked.

"I'd like t'go, too," Meg said. "My clothes should be dry by now."

"Me, too," Kathy said.

Their father smiled. "All right. You can all go. How 'bout you, Mis' Whitelock?"

"I feel real comfortable right where I am. Thanks anyway."

Skipper, who was outside, started to bark. Another car had turned into the boatyard.

"Now, I wonder who that might be," Mrs. Whitelock said.

There were hurried footsteps on the path. The screen door flew open, and Aunt Lavinia burst into the kitchen followed at a distance by Uncle Lester. Seeing Kathy on her father's knee, Aunt Lavinia rushed over to them. "Kathy, darling!" She knelt and put her arms around her. "My poor, poor baby!" Kathy drew back into her father's arms.

Chagrined at Kathy's response, Aunt Lavinia stood up and smoothed her dress. "Lavinia! This is a surprise!" Mr. Evans said.

"Surprise? You should've known we'd come! We started right out, soon as we heard on TV about the flood."

Uncle Lester, clearly uncomfortable, lingered just inside the door. "Well, well, well," he said with forced good humor. "You all appear to have survived the storm in good shape. But I see the old boat's gone."

Aunt Lavinia laid a hand on her brother's shoulder. "Tyler. I'm so sorry. Of course we'll take Kathy back with us. When you get back on your feet again, we'll—"

"Now hold on there, Lavinia." Mr. Evans put Kathy down and stood up. "Not so fast!"

"I know how you feel, Tyler. But it's the only thing to do. Think of the school problem. School starts in a few days, you know. Meg'll be—Tyler, you know it as well as I do. Meg's just too young and inexperienced to be trusted with the care of a small child."

"Mrs. Messick!" Mrs. Whitelock drew herself up to her full height and faced the other woman. "You can set your mind at ease 'bout Meg's bein' too young t'be trusted. She has better sense and more spunk than many grown women I know. Why, the things that girl's gone through, to have kept her spirits up and kept her head! She saw Kathy through a bad case of measles and nursed her real good. Dr. Bounds said so. And last night! The courage and resourcefulness she showed would've done credit to someone twice her age! As for her bein' away at school, I'm hopin' t'have the pleasure of lookin' after Kathy myself while Meg's gone. You see, they're all goin' t'live right here with me and the Captain. The whole family! So that settles that!"

Meg's father looked with disbelief at Mrs. Whitelock. A light was beginning to show in his eyes as he turned questioningly toward Captain Noah. "You in any way in agreement about this?"

Before Captain Noah had a chance to answer, Mrs. Whitelock spoke again. "I mean every word of what *I* said, Tyler. I haven't had a chance t'speak to Noah. But I'm sure he'll see the sense of it. You need a place t'live and you need someone t'keep an eye on Kathy while Meg's in school. We've a big old house that's gettin' too much for me t'care for, and—"

"The boys and I could clean the house on Saturdays and help with the cooking," Meg chimed in.

Lloyd nodded his head thoughtfully. "I could rake leaves this fall and shovel snow in the winter."

"I wouldn't mind weedin' your garden," Jamie offered, "if you'd show me how t'tell the weeds."

Mrs. Whitelock looked at her husband. "Noah, you're not sayin' much."

It was true, Meg thought. He hadn't said a word. She suddenly had a sinking sensation in her stomach. Maybe he wouldn't agree. Maybe the idea of having a bunch of kids in his house didn't appeal to him at all.

The Captain cleared his throat. "Bessie, you took me by surprise, is all. Jumped the gun, so t'speak, makin' such an offer without talkin' it over. But far as I can see, it looks like a good plan. Only way t'be sure is t'give it a try."

Meg breathed easier.

He turned to her father. "Bessie's right 'bout the house bein' too big for the two of us. It might be real good for us t'have young folks around. Durin' the winter, when the weather keeps us inside, we sort of rattle around."

"It'd just be till next summer, Noah. Then I reckon we can move onto the *Tessie* again. And I'll be wantin' t'pay you rent."

"Well, we can talk 'bout that later."

Aunt Lavinia was stunned. She had opened her mouth several times, but no words had come out. Finally she managed, "My lawyer and I have—"

Uncle Lester took her arm.

"Come on. Let's go, Lavinia. There's no place for you in this little scheme. We're not wanted here. Let's go home."

Captain Noah took a step toward him. "You'd do well t'head for home, Lester, but on your way I suggest you make a stop."

"A stop?"

"I suggest you make a stop at the police station and turn yourself in."

"What? You taken leave of your senses?"

"Don't reckon I have. You remember that little accident you had several weeks ago? You remember I went to see you, and you said you knew nothing about it, that it would be Lloyd's word against yours? Well, now I have another witness, an adult witness who will testify it was your car ran my pickup truck off the road and that you were driving it. We had time for some good talk yesterday."

"And who might this impressive witness be?" Uncle Lester asked sarcastically.

"Tyler, here."

"Tyler? Ha! He wouldn't have the intestinal fortitude to—"

"Lester, you're wrong about that," Mr. Evans said evenly. "Shootin' a few birds out o' season is one thing. Endangerin' people's lives is another. I reckon we were lucky the truck hit a tree, me and Lloyd. Could be we'd have rolled down that steep bank in the pickup, turned over, and lain there for hours."

As his father spoke Lloyd moved closer so that they were standing side by side.

Aunt Lavinia's face was drained of color. "Lester, you couldn't have . . . You didn't . . ."

"Lavinia, I want to make one thing clear. I had no idea it was your brother driving that truck and that's the God's truth! I thought it was just some country hick mindin' other people's business."

"Don't think that'll make a lot of difference in the sight of the law," Mr. Evans said.

Aunt Lavinia was staring at Uncle Lester with bulging eyes. "Lester, you mean to tell me you—you *deliberately* . . . you and your crummy huntin' buddies! No wonder you didn't want to come over here with me today! You were scared!" She fled from the house with a wail of outrage.

Uncle Lester started to follow, but Captain Noah stopped him again. "You should know, Lester, that Tyler and I were plannin' t'call the police in any case. If you turn yourself in, it should go better with you. Might make the difference 'tween goin' t'jail or not. You can offer t'pay for the damages to my truck. No doubt there'll be a whoppin' big fine for poachin', and I reckon you'll lose your driver's license. But it'd be worse for you the other way."

"This'll ruin my political career."

"And it should," Mr. Evans said. "You could've killed Lloyd. Or me."

Lloyd listened to his father with growing pride.

"You two really got me on the ropes, haven't you?" Uncle Lester sneered.

"You put yourself there, Lester."

Uncle Lester looked at Captain Noah, then back at his brother-in-law. Seeing their set faces he muttered, "Relatives! Bah!" and slammed out the door.

Lloyd grinned at his father. "Dad, you were great!"

"Thanks, son," Mr. Evans said, and their eyes met in real understanding.

Meg looked thoughtful. "You know, I almost feel sorry for Aunt Lavinia. I think maybe someday soon the whole family should go see her."

Jamie groaned.

"Just a short visit, Jamie."

With a chuckle Captain Noah reached for his cap. "It's time we did somethin' 'bout the *Tessie*. Anyone comin' with me?"

The ebbing tide had left the *Tessie*'s hull half out of water. Captain Noah eased the *J. P. Leonard* alongside, and Mr. Evans stepped onto her canted deck with a mooring line to make the *Leonard* fast. Lloyd, Jamie, and Meg followed.

Kathy was to stay on the *Leonard* with the Captain,

her father had decided. She watched the others for a moment, then her eyes strayed to the top of the mainmast. She let out a squeal. "There she is! There's Scaredy! See?"

Everyone looked up. Near the top of the mast Scaredy clung, afraid to budge. She began to mew pitifully.

"I'll get her for you, Kat," Jamie said.

"All right. Go ahead," his father said. "Only be careful."

Jamie shinnied up the mast, pried Scaredy's claws loose, and put her over his shoulder. "Ouch! Quit clawing me, cat!" he complained as he slid toward the deck.

Lloyd took Scaredy from Jamie's shoulder and passed her to Kathy, who settled herself contentedly with the kitten on her lap. Just then the buzz of an outboard motor directed everyone's attention toward the shore. Meg saw a skiff heading in their direction. In its stern sat a youth with reddish-brown hair. Meg's heart began to pound. It had to be Peter Dawson. It had to be!

He pulled alongside the *Tessie*, smiling his familiar lopsided grin, and doused the motor. Lloyd handed him a line.

"Thanks, Lloyd." He made the skiff fast. "Hello, everybody! Hi, Gramps! Got home yesterday. Thought I'd come down and see about you. I figured with all the storm damage you could use some help. Never guessed the *Tessie*'d go for a sail, though." He smiled up at Meg.

"Nice t'see you, Peter," Captain Noah said. "How 'bout your folks? They comin' down?"

"Yep. They'll be here on Monday. Dad couldn't get away today. I hitched."

"Well, there's plenty t'be done, as you can plainly see. Right now we're off-loading the *Tessie*."

As Peter came aboard, Mr. Evans gave him a friendly

nod. "We can use your help. That's for certain. Meg, you'd best come below with me and help decide what needs takin' ashore. You know best where things are. We'll hand what we can salvage up to the boys."

The interior of the cabin was a sorry sight. Only about three feet of water remained above the floorboards, but as it receded it had left a film of mud behind. All the family's belongings—books, bedding, and clothes—were a soggy mess. Meg's salad bowl was still voyaging around the cabin. Her father waded in to rescue it. With the bowl on her lap Meg sat on the companionway steps, discouraged by what she saw. "Your beautiful paneling, Dad! It's covered with mud!"

"It looks bad, all right. But the hull doesn't appear t've taken much hurt. We'll pump her out, then haul her over to the boatyard. She should shape up pretty good, I reckon. There'll be plenty of time t'work on her this winter."

With a sigh Meg started down the companionway prepared to wade through the water and pull clothes out of the hanging lockers. She had barely wet her feet when she heard Lloyd call, "Meg! Meg, come up here!"

She wasted no time in scrambling out on deck.

"Look!" Peter said, pointing toward the Bay.

Meg saw two great birds flying toward them low. Their long necks were gracefully extended, and their wings, seven feet from tip to tip, slowly fanned the air. A dagger of jet black ran from black bill to eye. Their neatly tucked-up legs were reddish orange. Other than that, they were snowy white.

"Wild swans!" Peter exclaimed.

"The first," Lloyd said.

The swans banked in a slow circle, headed for Barren

Island and the plentiful supply of their favorite marsh grass which grew there. As they turned, the sun shone through their wings, making them almost transparent against the brightness of the September sky.

Peter stood close to Meg and his hand closed over one of hers. She laid her other hand caressingly on the *Tessie*'s old weather-beaten mast. She was glad the swans had come back to the marshes and shallow waters of the Bay, back to Chesapeake country. And she was glad, more than glad, that Peter Dawson stood beside her at this moment and held her hand firmly in his.